CRAVING BEAUTY

WYLDER TALES, VOLUME ONE

JENNIFER SILVERWOOD

Craving Beauty (A Wylder Tale: Volume 1) 2023 Edition by Jennifer Silverwood Published by SilverWoodSketches www.jennifersilverwood.com

Cover Design and Formatting by Qamber Designs
Map by Daniel's Maps
Edited by R.J. Locksley

ISBN: 979-8-3966-1470-3

I wouldn't be writing today without the support and encouragement of the people who continue to keep from becoming a hedge witch of the woods. To each of you who helped bring this story to life in both incarnations, you know who you are. If I could bottle magick for you, I'd make all your wishes come true.

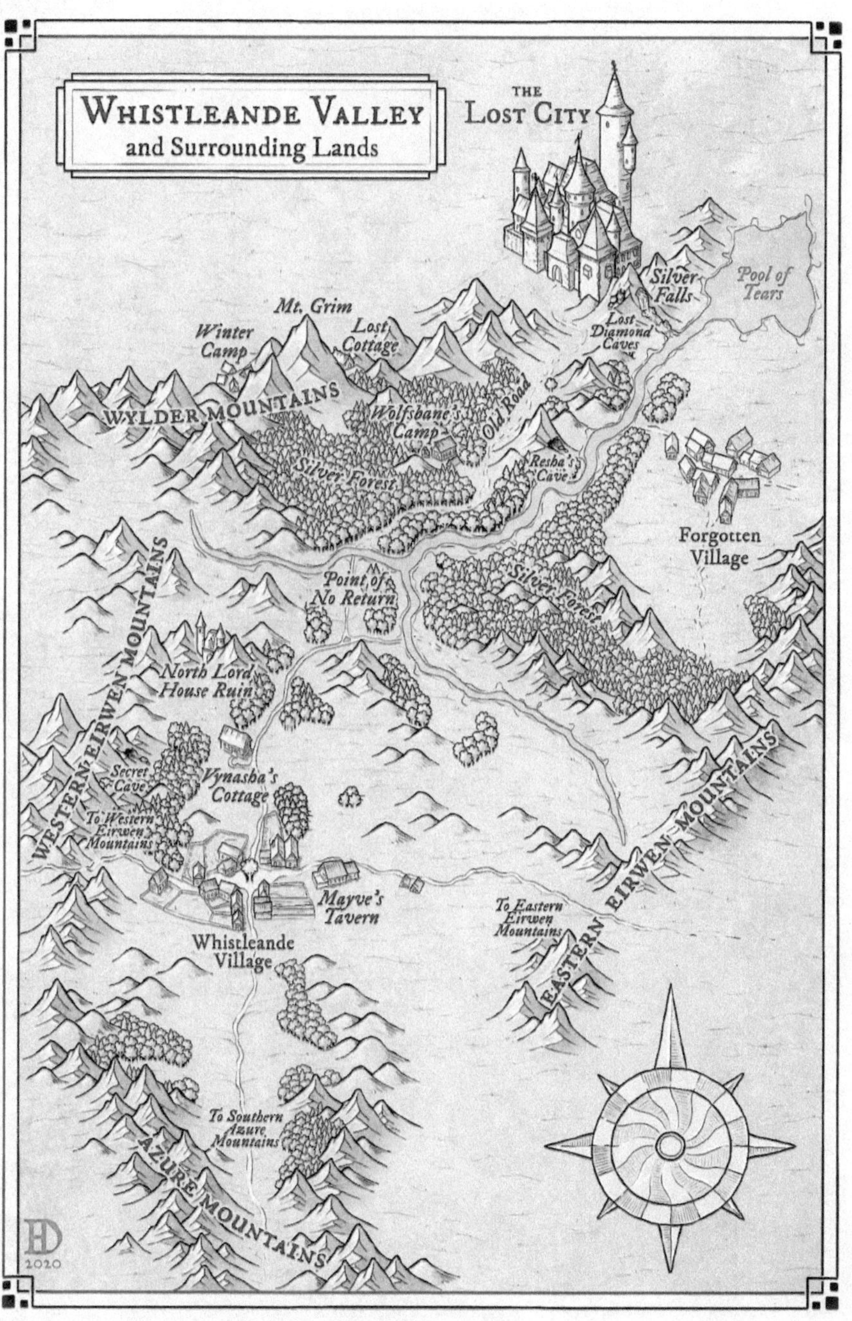

WHISTLEANDE VALLEY
and Surrounding Lands
THE LOST CITY
Silver Falls
Pool of Tears
Mt. Grim
Winter Camp
Lost Cottage
Lost Diamond Caves
WYLDER MOUNTAINS
Wolfsbane's Camp
Old Road
Silver Forest
Resha's Cave
Forgotten Village
Silver Forest
Point of No Return
WESTERN EIRWEN MOUNTAINS
North Lord House Ruin
Secret Cave
Vynasha's Cottage
To Western Eirwen Mountains
EASTERN EIRWEN MOUNTAINS
Mayve's Tavern
To Eastern Eirwen Mountains
Whistleande Village
To Southern Azure Mountains
AZURE MOUNTAINS
2020

Once Upon a Nightmare

THE LANDS TO the far north had not always been locked within a season of endless winter.

Once, I was not the monster they say I am.

A memory persisted, in the minds of his people, of a time when spring and magick had overflown the land with abundance. Until Queen Soraya found her revenge and cut their land and its people from the outside world. What had seemed a reckoning became their doom.

Once, they looked to me for hope rather than with fear.

The Beast should not have listened to the enchantress and her pithy lies. He should have been strong enough for his people. He should have…

"Master?" interrupted the weak shadow of a voice. All the servants were but whispers now.

"Enter," he replied in his deep, growling voice. The magick forced him into this form, the one that made servants quake and lesser beasts flee in terror. He leaned his clawed hands over the balcony railing overlooking the Wylderlands beyond.

"Master," the servant began again, close as the old one dared. "There are whispers in the walls again. The tapestries say the old blood has been born anew."

His breath passed fanged lips in great, heated clouds. "I thought you knew better than to listen to mutterings of the dead, Odym."

The castle sat atop the highest of the surrounding peaks. It had been built into the mountain, delving deeply as both fortress and mine for precious gems. The grand mansions sprawling past the fortress were empty now, naught but a refuge for ghosts.

We will all be ghosts before the end.

"Master," the old servant spoke again, his voice a shadow of the soldier he'd once been, "*she* has been whispering to me of the prophecy once again as well."

Stone cracked beneath the Beast's great clawed hands. He bit back a snarl at the thought of their former queen. Her spirit lingered along with her damned curse.

I should have never listened to her promises. It is my fault we must linger unto dust. My fault…

"Master? Have we not suffered long enough? Mightn't we seek the curse breaker?"

The Beast growled as he whirled on the old servant, bitter words at the tip of his tongue. Until his gaze fell upon the gilded arch waiting in the room. The mirror stood empty and silent, just as it had the last age.

Once, they had been so close to leaving this cursed land, to returning home where they belonged. He came here to remember the price of his pride. His people continued to pay the toll.

Odym was little more than a shade now, and he had faded far too much in recent years. The old soldier lifted his hands in supplication to the Beast now. "We may not survive another year. You know this."

The Beast heard others roaming the castle levels far below. Ever was he aware of the cost and the price. Could what remained of them indeed last much longer? Or should he let them all fade to legend? Revenge had seemed sweet at first, but he had forgotten much in his endless need for reckoning.

The Beast turned back to the oncoming snowfall and bowed his head as he rumbled, "Send out the call."

To the one who would be helpless to answer, he only hoped she could one day forgive him.

Chapter One

A Girl Called Beauty

THE SKIES SHIFTED from a violet haze into a glassy gray sheen. Winter had been long and hard, and tiny snowflakes clung to the valley. The village of Whistleande was eerily silent, compared to streets that had filled with laughter and song before the war. Shopkeepers were wary of strangers and struggling to make ends meet. It was near one of these shops that her father and brother packed the rest of the supplies they'd need for the long journey through the Wylder Mountains.

The villagers whispered Old Ced must have finally gone mad if the merchant was daring the forbidden road north. No one went north, not when all knew the Wylder Mountains were cursed. That his newly returned son, Ceddrych the younger, had agreed to accompany him had also puzzled the villagers. Few of the sons of Whistleande had returned from their king's pointless war south. Of those who returned, much was expected to help rebuild what was lost. Why brave such a hazardous journey after everything, unless the worst had happened, and the family had fallen to ruin?

Vynasha had overheard the whispers and barely checked her sharp tongue on her errands to town. Her brother had confided the truth to her. What few assets had lingered in their coffers after Father's family fell to ruin were depleted from the war. Old Ced had no choice, not if they were to survive another lean winter. Away they must go, and what better way to change their fortunes than by traveling roads the family had once ruled over?

The rest of their sisters remained ignorant of the truth. The eldest, Tamyra, was too busy raising her son at Grandmother Mayve's tavern and hadn't arrived yet to see the men off. The two middle sisters, Adriaa and Iona, fought behind their father's broad back over a string of amber beads.

"Iona, your complexion is too dark for amber." Adriaa tossed her blond braid over her shoulder. "They look far better on me, anyway."

Iona's green eyes flashed. "Give them back, you vain hag! You just want them to impress Roshem when it's clear he loves me."

Vynasha cringed and tightened her grip on her skirts to contain her temper. It would only be worse for her later if she shouted or slapped her sisters. And oh, how she longed to damn the consequences and put an end to their selfish bickering. But Ceddrych had made her promise to behave, especially while they were gone. This was not the way her brother would want her to act, not with him and Father about to embark on their longest trading journey yet.

Old Ced's boots squished through the muddy street as he added the final sack to the back end of the cart. From the set of his brow, he was doing his best to ignore her sisters' shrieks. No help would come from him, of course. Father barely acknowledged them of late and only spoke with his namesake when pressed. Vynasha stepped off the boardwalk onto the muddy street, avoiding the source of her father's grumbling at the back of the wagon.

A taller man in a gray cloak stood on the opposite end beside the horses, checking over their tack and gear. Ceddrych had already said a proper goodbye before the family came to the village earlier that morn. Vynasha was too old to be trailing her brother's cloak, a woman grown. This didn't stop her from reaching a calloused hand to clutch the scratchy gray wool.

Ceddrych bowed his head slightly before pulling her hand free of his cloak and threading his fingers with hers. He turned, and his hazel eyes brightened as he met her gaze, though he did not smile. For a moment, they stood in the cool, muddy street, together as they always had been, and watched their breath escape in misty clouds. "It'll be summer, early autumn at the latest, before we return."

Vynasha nodded. She already knew this. She was the youngest of her siblings, but Ceddrych claimed she was the smartest, and Vynasha clung to his faith in her. "You'll write the first chance you find," she insisted. They had exchanged letters during the war, and often, his words were the only reason she hadn't run away after him.

"Next tavern we come to," Ceddrych agreed. He squeezed her hand even tighter and pulled her back to join the others on the boardwalk.

"Time we were off now!" came their father's barking tone.

Vynasha buried her face in Ceddrych's cloak, inhaling his comforting scent one last time. His arms drew her in tighter, and she knew his shudder was not from the cold. Same as she knew his eyes didn't sting with tears from the wind.

"We should leave before losing any more daylight," Old Ced's gruff voice interrupted.

Vynasha stood back and stiffened as her father approached, anger lingering behind his empty eyes. Ceddrych didn't let go of her hand.

Their father lifted his chin and settled his blank gaze on her. "I expect to find everything in order when we return. See Cousin Stye at the tavern should one of your sisters' suitors propose a contract."

Vynasha's mouth twisted into a grimace. "Farewell, Father."

Old Ced grunted something under his breath before turning on his heel and marching over to kiss her sisters' cheeks.

Vynasha exchanged a glance with Ceddrych. "He's still angry with me for refusing to join the bloody nunnery," she said. It wasn't fair that none of the others had been given such an ultimatum. But Tamyra was an independent widow, and Adriaa and Iona had at least four suitors between them.

Ceddrych sighed, but he didn't speak the truth they both knew, the real reason no man in Whistleande would pursue Vynasha's hand in marriage.

Witch, they had called Old Ced's second wife. Only a witch could make roses bloom in the middle of winter, as her mother had and Vynasha could still.

Ceddrych's voice pulled her back from her dark thoughts, as usual. "You'll do just fine, managing things until we return. Now, enough about our miserable family. I did many questionable things to find my way home to you, Ash. I *will* come back again, hopefully with a small fortune in tow." He waited for her grudging nod before a spark lit his eyes and warmed her heart.

"So long as you promise to come home, that's all that matters." She slipped her arm around his waist, and the hilt of his sword dug into her side.

His arm about her shoulders tightened. "I know Old Ced hasn't been the same since we lost Wynyth. I think it was difficult for him to face us after losing the last of his fortune with this war."

Vynasha sucked in a sharp breath at the mention of their father's failure and Wynyth's death. Old Ced never spoke of her, but they all noted the fact his hair had turned snow white. There had been fear mixed in with sorrow ever after as they struggled to help their father rebuild his business. Both subsequent losses had become the final wind that scattered their family.

Ceddrych turned her round so that his hands were clasped over her shoulders. His eyes spoke volumes his words could not. "Ash," he finally said. "I'm sorry I'm leaving you alone with them again."

She waved away his words and turned to look at the fields bordering the village. "You know I can take care of myself."

"Yes, but they won't take care of you."

Tamyra and little Wyll arrived as Vynasha finally pulled from Ceddrych's embrace.

He was going to be the death of her, she thought, as he kissed Adriaa and Iona on the cheek then wrapped his arms around their oldest sibling, Tamyra. He kissed little Wyll on top of his curly head with gentle words. "You look after them while I'm gone, little man?"

Vynasha gripped the side of the cart as she watched her brother give his farewells to the rest of their family. It had been repainted to show "Whistleande Wares," and a fine tarp now covered the crates within. The road would be long and dangerous, and Vynasha couldn't shake the feeling that this journey was a mistake.

Father gave Tamyra instructions from his perch atop the wagon seat. "Cousin Stye will come round now and again to help with repairs should you need him. Your sisters can do the cooking and cleaning at the house and the tavern as you need aid."

"Yes, Father," Tamyra replied.

Vynasha wanted to scream at him, both of them, for leaving her behind again. Adriaa and Iona would not help with any chores. They would spend more time in town than on the farm. How could she do this alone now that Tamyra was living above the tavern?

"Ash." Ceddrych lifted her chin until she was forced to meet his hazel eyes. "It's only for a season. Remember, we'll be rich as kings soon. We'll start over again, together."

"Together," Vynasha whispered.

The moments after passed a blur behind her tears. Tamyra's arm was suddenly about her shoulders, pulling her back onto the boardwalk as she drew Wyll aside with her other hand. "Come, I've got you, little wolf."

Vynasha watched the wagon pull down the main street until it was no longer in sight, long after Adriaa and Iona began the long walk home.

"Can we go with Aunty Ash to the big house now?" Little Wyll piped up, startling them both.

Tamyra glanced up from beneath her long lashes. "I don't know if we should, dear. Although Cousin Stye could manage for one night, I suppose…"

Vynasha surprised herself by smiling. Her eldest sister had married the village blacksmith just before the war broke out, barely long enough to make little Wyll. Soon after Tamyra had learned Wyll would never meet his father, she'd moved into the tavern with Grandmother Mayve.

Vynasha squeezed her older sister's smaller hand and looked down into her blue eyes. "Thank you. I don't think I could bear a night alone with Adriaa and Iona just now."

"Indeed not." Tamyra laughed and shook her head so her short curls were freed from her white ruffled cap. "Come along, then. I'll help you make supper."

Vynasha wrapped her arms around her sister's neck as they began the journey home.

Dinner within the farmhouse near the forest passed in near-blessed peace. Until Tamyra and Wyll retreated upstairs. That was when the battle began anew.

"Vynasha, have you finished boiling that water yet? I simply *must* bathe tonight, before Roshem comes calling on the morrow," Iona insisted.

Vynasha froze before the fireplace she'd been stoking afresh and spoke as calmly as she could manage. "This hot water is for *Tam* and *Wyll*, not you."

Iona turned puce beneath her dusky cheeks. "Why are you serving them, *Beauty*?"

Vynasha's grip froze over the iron kettle she'd settled over the hearth at Ceddrych's special nickname for her. No matter how often she'd protested she was anything but a beauty. "Don't call me that," she nearly growled back.

Iona stood and casually stalked nearer, a cruel smile tugging at her lovely face. "Not so brave now that Ced's not here to defend you."

Ceddrych hated that nickname. It's what everyone in the village called their father, and son or not, he wanted little to do with his namesake.

It was the final straw.

Vynasha left the kettle on its hook and rose to her feet. She was taller than Iona now, at least. "Don't be a bitch just because Roshem would rather marry Adriaa instead of you."

Her head snapped to the side and her face stung where Iona had slapped her. Vynasha clenched her fists and refused to fight back.

It wouldn't be fair, she reminded herself. Not when the same buzzing tingling flushed hot in her veins, the way it often did as she tended Mother's roses. "It wouldn't be fair," she muttered under her breath.

"What's the witch saying now?" Adriaa's voice drawled lazily from where she sat before Wynyth's old dresser.

Iona didn't take her cat-like gaze from Vynasha as she sneered. "She's clearly mad and would do better to keep her mouth *shut* before her betters."

Adriaa arched one brow and continued to brush through her long blond tresses. "You are only jealous, Iona. Jealous as you always have been. Do not think I haven't known about all your little plans, the lies you convinced others to spread. Perhaps if you and Vynasha could both be silent long enough, I would find a place for you in my household when I am named queen."

"You evil cow!" Iona grabbed the nearest object she could, a wooden vase filled with Vynasha's roses, and threw them across the room.

"No!" Vynasha's knees smarted as she fell to the floor beside Wynyth's delicately carved vase. There were few of her mother's possessions left after Father auctioned so much of their remaining wealth.

Iona held her belly as she laughed at Vynasha's pain. "Oh, good God, you actually care about that old witch's trash?"

Vynasha clutched the broken pieces to her chest. Her skin buzzed hotter, and something deeply dark and twisted struggled to claw its way up her throat. Hot tears spilled over her cheeks. "Do you *honestly* think the king would marry either of you?" Vynasha snapped. "Our house was stripped of land and titles, and now we have nothing to our name. Father has ruined us, and he stole what silver my mother carried. You have *no right*, no right to touch my mother's things!"

Iona's wicked sneer faded as Vynasha stumbled to her feet. Vynasha advanced on her with fire in her eyes as Iona retreated, sputtering, "Your mother was a no one from *nothing*, and it's her fault Father lost his head. She bewitched him, just as you have bewitched Ceddrych!"

Adriaa didn't bother to get up, only pressed her shoe to the open bloodred rose at her feet. With the awful crunch, Vynasha flinched. "If only you had gone to the nunnery when you had the chance, witch."

Vynasha pushed out a trembling breath. The dark thing inside her longed to slash and bite and maim.

"*It wouldn't be fair,*" her mother's voice whispered in her head.

"Where are you going, witch?" Adriaa called.

Vynasha ignored the way the snow soaked through her house slippers. She'd forgotten her boots and her coat. But the darkness still clawed at her skin, begging to be set free. She didn't dare turn back.

Not until she was safe in their special place. She and Ceddrych had hidden away so often over the years. They kept sleeping furs, some rations, and supplies to make a fire for nights when they didn't want to go home. While Ceddrych was away at war, Vynasha practically lived in this cave during the warmer seasons.

With the onset of winter, the cave was bitterly cold.

She barely felt it with her blood still running hot as she wrapped herself in the furs that still smelled like the only person who loved her unconditionally.

Vynasha cradled the broken pieces of her mother's wooden vase to her heart and cried herself to sleep.

CHAPTER TWO

A Voice in the Wind

"**C**OME," THE NAMELESS voice whispered in her dreams.

Vynasha shivered as invisible hands pushed aside her furs and traced over her skin.

"*Come to me,*" the voice rumbled with a distant thunder.

Cold, sickly terror woke her, followed by a desperate urge that demanded she leave the broken pieces of her mother behind.

"*Yes… come now,*" the voice sang with the wind, carrying snow and the heavy scent of ash through the edge of the forest.

"*Run,*" the voice urged with something close to fear beneath the deep tones.

Vynasha ignored the sting in her toes as she worked blood through her limbs and ran as quickly as she could through the gathering snow.

She tripped over roots as she broke through the tree line. The sky ahead glowed with unnatural light. Black clouds covered the stars.

"*Faster,*" the voice hissed.

Vynasha scrambled up the rise blocking her view of the house. Ashes stung as they alighted on her skin. Smoke greeted her long before the sight of roaring flames consumed her vision.

She couldn't breathe.

The flames licked hungrily over the outer frame of the two-storied house, but the roof was obscured by the thick black smoke she'd caught traces of in the sky.

A voice screamed through the flames.

Tamyra. Wyll.

"Oh, God," Vynasha gasped and coughed as she ran to the porch and froze once more. She turned to the clumps of snow and, grabbing fistfuls, drenched herself in the drifts. "Please," she prayed as she stepped onto the porch and opened the front door.

Patches of floor were yet clear, yet the fire must have begun here.

"Asha!" a small voice cried somewhere above the creak and roar of hungry flame.

"*Hurry! Upstairs,*" the strange voice growled as snow swirled through the open door behind her.

Vynasha ignored the wood peeling back in thick molten globs overhead as she ran up the stairs and ducked below smoke through the hall to the attic room. Fresh ashes showered over her wet skin as she kicked open the door and flinched at the sudden surge of more flames.

Vynasha covered her face and ran into the room. "Wyll!"

It was dark in the attic, thick with black smoke. A whimper sounded just ahead, beneath a fallen beam.

Vynasha crawled over and sobbed as she found Tamyra and Wyll trapped beneath.

A blackened hand clasped her wrist, and Tamyra's bold blue eyes silently pleaded with her.

Vynasha nodded quickly and scrambled around to find Wyll clutching his mother's neck, sobbing with desperate breaths.

"Wyll, please." Vynasha coughed as she pulled her nephew from his mother. The stink of burning flesh overwhelmed her senses as she stumbled over the beam and back through the attic door.

"Mama!" Wyll screamed.

Vynasha flinched as more flames dripped from the walls in hideous curls. "Hold on to me, Wyll!"

The stairs crumpled moments after they reached the landing. Vynasha screamed as a fire singed her arms. She bowed her head over Wyll's and followed the promise of snow just as the roof and the walls caved in.

"*A little farther*," the voice in the wind crooned.

Vynasha collapsed in a heap, Wyll in her lap, the instant they reached the untouched barn.

Saints, please keep the ashes from touching the barn, she silently prayed as she leaned against the barn wall, her nephew cradled in her arms.

She still couldn't breathe. The fire lingered in her chest, and each breath was a new agony.

"Oh, God, Ceddrych," she whispered. "What can we do now?"

Her voice did not sound like hers. She doubted if she would ever feel like the girl who ran away to the woods again. Not as she held her nephew's burned face against her bloody palm. Vynasha forced her attention from the house to Wyll.

He looked dully past her with glazed blue eyes, Tamyra's eyes.

"Wyll?" Her voice was hoarse, and the howling winds beyond the barn nearly overwhelmed the sound. "Wyll, please don't leave me. Don't leave me here alone."

She bit her cracked lip and smoothed brittle curls from his blistered forehead. Wyll didn't flinch. Fighting a sob, she leaned closer, pleading, "Please, Wyll… I'm so afraid."

Yet her nephew did not blink or turn to her and smile with his mother's sweet grin. The coal black of his eyes consumed the blue, and Vynasha froze as a rattling breath escaped his parted lips.

A broken moan escaped her as she shook him. "Wyll! God, open your eyes, *please*! Please don't leave me alone," she begged.

Vynasha burrowed her face against his neck, buried her hot tears in his tattered nightshirt. Wyll wouldn't open his eyes, no matter how loudly she called. He would never smile at her again. That was when she knew he was gone and she was truly alone.

Vynasha rocked with him beneath the barn overhang, within the snowdrifts, and whispered against his skin. She uttered forbidden words her mother had whispered to her deep in the night in that strange musical tongue Vynasha had half forgotten.

She remembered it now as the darkness stirred beneath her skin.

"*We must be careful, my starling,*" Mother had made her promise. "*Be oh, so careful. To give life, we must always sacrifice.*"

Vynasha's tears dried as she continued to whisper the words she spoke to Wynyth's roses. As the fire died and only smoke lingered. As the torches of the villagers steadily approached the long road to what remained.

"*Vynasha,*" the voice crooned to her in the wind, a song of sorrow and mourning.

The little body in her arms did not grow cold as it should have.

It shuddered against her in spasms.

Vynasha squeezed her eyes tightly shut as the little hands clenched her arms in a tight grasp.

Wyll sucked in a hoarse gasp as he breathed new life.

The little boy whimpered and then spoke as though back from a long sleep. "Asha?"

Vynasha pulled back with a sob as she found Wyll's blue eyes open and taking in the world around them with wonder. The melted half of his face was not fully healed. The burns were severe but would not claim his life. This much she knew.

The same way Vynasha knew how to keep roses blooming in the dead of winter.

The way her mother, Wynyth, had taught her long ago.

She wept now for her mother and for Tamyra and Ceddrych. Yes, she even wept for Old Ced and her sisters. She wept for herself and clung to the only family she had left and wondered how she would find the strength to continue.

"*Come to me soon,*" the voice called again, but it was little more than a distant rasp.

Vynasha held her nephew closer and ignored the call.

WINTER

SPRING

SUMMER

AUTUMN

CHAPTER THREE

A Promise Broken

THE ROSES WERE finally ready to bring to market in the village of Whistleande. Fresh dew lingered in the garden, coating her blooms that grew in abundance over the ashes that had once been their home. Fitting, she supposed, that her family helped give life to the blossoms which helped provide for what remained.

Vynasha cupped one snow-white bud with her fingers and whispered in her mother's tongue to the bound petals. Upon command, they slowly unraveled to reveal their red, magenta, and lavender-gray hues.

With a sigh of satisfaction, she removed her hands and sank into the grass. Winds swooped down from the nearby mountains to tug her shawl from her shoulders while it tugged wisps from her waist-length braid, as though pulling her north.

"*Come,*" the wind whispered in a familiar voice.

Vynasha clenched her jaw as she faced the imposing peaks. "He's coming home," she hissed back.

"*It'll be summer, early autumn at the latest,*" Ceddrych had promised her what seemed a year ago, the season everything died.

"*He will not return,*" the voice taunted with another gust of northerly winds.

"Go to hell." Vynasha's cheek pulled with her scowl, pinching slightly where the worst burns lined the side of her face. She brought her shawl back over her head and set to gathering the rest of her roses into her basket.

The wind did not reply.

The sun never beat heavily within the mountains. Leaves of amber, scarlet, and gold danced over the path beyond the ruins that served as her rose garden. Vynasha hadn't intended to plant there, but Wynyth once told her that roses had a mind of their own. And in the aftermath of their family's ruin, Vynasha hadn't the heart to dig through the ashes for her sisters' remains. What lingering stone remained she'd used as part of a new garden wall.

Grandmother Mayve hadn't understood it. Then again, she hadn't understood Vynasha's need to live in the repurposed barn, nor Wyll's refusal to live apart from his young aunt.

Clouds gathered overhead with the promise of the approaching winter. Autumn never lasted long, even in the valley. The harvest was nearly upon them. What few vegetables they'd coaxed from the hard earth were kept for eating. The roses were their only crop Vynasha could manage alone.

Vynasha blinked against the sudden drizzle of rain that dusted her head. She mustn't waste any more time if she wanted to reach the village before the storm broke. Cousin Stye would be expecting her.

She pulled her shawl closer as she darted through the open door of their home.

The dying flicker of the early-morning fire, now smoking within the central pit they called a hearth, greeted her. She scowled at the charred wood. Wyll hadn't been able to stoke the fire himself today. Vynasha set her basket down and passed their only remaining horse, with a quick caress to his nose, and whispered, "Dragos."

"Asha?" The small voice gave her pause, and Vynasha turned to the single bed she shared with her nephew. Wyll's fever-bright eyes were fixed upon her, and it took everything she could muster to force a lop-sided smile on her face. The scars kept her smile from stretching across both cheeks as it once had.

"That's my Beauty," Ceddrych had called her.

What would you think of me now, brother?

Vynasha shoved the familiar bitterness down as she limped slightly to her nephew's side. "You should be resting."

She brushed Wyll's mop of black curls from his eyes. He was so young, *too* young to have struggled as they had the past year. He was the only one she had pulled out of the flames in time. But he was considerably weakened and prone to illness with each coming season.

There had been dark days when Vynasha wondered if she hadn't been selfish in saving Wyll's life the way she had. She wondered if his fevers and his weakened heart were not somehow her fault. She wondered if he would survive the winter.

Wyll sighed against her touch. "I had the nightmare," he whispered.

Vynasha nodded as she continued to run her fingers through his hair. It had grown in slowly and patchy where the burns had been worse. It was a miracle he had hair at all.

"A miracle," the villagers had said after finding them huddled in the snow outside the ruined cottage. Vynasha had shuddered at this, knowing full well what could happen if they learned the truth.

Vynasha and Wyll often shared the same nightmare in the long nights since the fire. Only in her dreams, Vynasha was often bound to a post within the pyre.

"To give life requires sacrifice, little starling," Mother had said.

"It's going to storm soon," Vynasha finally said aloud. "I need to go to the village before it hits the valley."

Wyll nodded, and his fingers brushed over her arm. "Hurry? I don't want to be alone." And in his blue eyes, she saw her sister Tamyra.

She bent down to kiss his forehead and squeezed her eyes shut to fight back tears. "I will," she promised upon standing. "I'll always come back, Wyll." This was a promise she'd die to keep, too. She wouldn't leave him the way the rest of her family...

Ceddrych, why haven't you come home?

Vynasha couldn't bear to meet Wyll's eye as she fed the fire pit. Pretending confidence and hope for Wyll had been more difficult with each season. And if she couldn't raise his spirits before winter's tide, neither of them would survive.

She'd never thought much of death before the fire had claimed their family's lives, the tragedy that had left her scarred and limping as she reached for her basket of roses. Maybe it would have been better if she had simply laid down with Tamyra and Wyll that night. Maybe she should have taken Grandmother Mayve's offer and lived above the tavern.

And be forced to endure their stares every day?

Vynasha placed her shawl over her head then covered her harvest with a linen cloth. "Stop thinking about it," she admonished as she hefted her basket over her elbow and once more took the long path to the village.

Whistleande had once been the most thriving village in the kingdom. Built in the center of a valley tucked away by the Azur Mountains to the south and the forbidden Wylder Mountains to the north, it had served as a center of trade for all the people who lived there.

Foreigners in their extravagant cloaks, bearing cloth of colorful weaves, had come from neighboring fiefdoms and kingdoms beyond the eastern Eirwen Mountains and the flatlands beyond. Vynasha's father once said that her mother had come from those faraway plains.

Mist drizzled before her eyes, revealing the chimneys fixed into roofs and dwellings below. Whistleande looked much the same as it always had. Before the war, the streets had been crowded with merchants and farmers, trading their wares and crops for goods. Troublemakers wearing dark cloaks and cruel expressions wove through the hubbub, and elders held court on benches along the outside of the Commons, where all matters were decided. Now, the streets felt hollow, and the village was but a shell of its former self.

Just like me, she thought with a vicious twist of her lips.

Absent were the traders who usually lined the streets, the corners with wagons full of commodities, and fewer farmers and troublemakers were milling about each year. Instead, once-young, able-bodied men had been traded for a few scarred and lined faces. Elders stared at the muddy street before their benches in a morose daydream because their sons had never come home. Many buildings were falling into disrepair, and even more housed half-starved faces she often caught looking out from the shadows.

Grandmother Mayve's tavern had passed on to the grimier hands of a distant cousin two months ago, known to his patrons as Stye. Vynasha could no longer remember the details of their connection, nor could she recall his true name. She would ever be grateful to and furious with Stye for taking over and then neglecting her grandmother's establishment. Mayve hadn't survived the burden of the sudden death of her only son and most of his children.

Was it selfish of me to keep Wyll at home instead of letting her keep him here?

Mayve's Tavern was only a faded painting of its former glory, and the old sign swung on a single remaining chain. While most businesses in the village failed, a piece of her grandmother remained.

After scraping her boots against the steps, Vynasha ducked through the heavy wooden door and pushed her way inside.

Pipes played from the far corner of the lamp-lit bar. Brooding men and women sat at the tables as maids served them their morning meals. Most had become permanent dwellers over the last several years, as fewer and fewer traders dared the passes leading into their poor, forgotten kingdom.

As she made her way over to where Stye stood, laughing behind the bar, several looked up at her entrance and flinched. Vynasha pushed her rain-soaked shawl back as she approached. She had seen her reflection in enough broken mirrors to know whatever beauty she might have once possessed was gone thanks to her scars.

He called me Beauty…

What would Ceddrych think if he saw her now? No matter how she wore her hair or cloak, the scars on the side of her face and neck were a constant reminder of what she was.

The remaining troublemakers in Whistleande kept residence upon the stools lining the bar. Their whispers stilled, and their cruel mouths turned down into sneers at her appearance.

Let them bloody look.

Stye's sudden laugh distracted them so she could slip past unmolested. "I tell you gents, poor Rolvyn could barely stand on his own bootless feet after that much ale! And I'd like to see any of you try to do better. But of course, there's no chance in the devil's hell you'd make it." Shouts of protests met Stye's challenge, and his eyes gleamed at the coin the men threw in as wagers on his bet. Mugs were soon filled to the brim in exchange.

"To Mayve!" They toasted the grimy portrait of her grandmother displayed over Stye's shoulder before drowning in the rich amber liquid together.

"Come along while they're distracted." Stye was suddenly by her side, a meaty hand at her elbow as he led her through the back room with a quick, "Poz, watch those laggards for me!"

Once the door shut behind them, Stye wiped his face with the rag on his shoulder and scowled at the kitchen maids.

One poor girl dropped her ladle upon sight of Vynasha.

"Don't you dare start blubbering, wench! She's family, not the devil's own," Stye growled. "Go serve that slosh before I have a mind to teach you better manners."

The maid nodded and tripped over her skirts on her way past them into the tavern.

Vynasha held still to the shadows until Stye had settled into a chair before the hearth.

"Don't just stand there, Beauty, come let's have a look at your harvest," Stye said with a sad smile.

Vynasha bristled and bit her tongue. Only Ceddrych was allowed to call her Beauty.

She glanced at the oblivious cook, an old gray-hair who'd been at the tavern since Mayve established it decades ago.

"Don't worry about old Wylma. She won't trouble us. You know that. Now, *sit*, girl. We don't have all day."

Vynasha did her best to hide her limp as she settled into the opposite chair and set her basket on the stone floor.

Stye gasped as she unveiled the roses. They appeared as fresh as the moment she'd cut them with Ceddrych's knife. They would remain fresh for weeks, or so long as they could hold against the misery of Stye's customers. Whistleande Village had a poor habit of sucking the life out of beautiful things.

"Amazing," Stye muttered. "Even prettier than your mother's, you know."

Vynasha met his dark eyes. Their exchanges never lasted very long, not since Grandmother Mayve's passing. Vynasha couldn't look at Stye without a familiar guilt wrecking her nerves.

My fault. All my fault.

Aloud, she dared speak. "Did you know my mother?"

"Wynyth was kind to me." Stye ran reverent fingers over the rose petals. "Did you know she convinced Mayve to take me in?"

Vynasha picked at the fingerless gloves disguising the worst of her burns. "I… I'm sorry for Mayve," she choked.

Stye frowned and looked up as though startled. "Sorry? Beauty, what could you possibly feel sorry for? Mayve's old heart couldn't handle the grief, 'tis all. None of what has befallen your family is your fault. You know this, I hope?"

Vynasha pulled her cloak over her head. "May I take our usual portion now?"

Stye braced his hands on his knees. "You know, you and Wyll are always welcome to live here. It would be the least I could do for the kindness your family has shown me."

"I mustn't keep Wyll waiting." She stood to her feet too quickly. She couldn't stop looking at her roses, anywhere but Stye's concerned and kindly face. He was not quite the harsh man he presented to the others, but he was too close to her family. He did not see her or Wyll as the villagers saw them.

"Vynasha, you have friends," Stye insisted, going so far as to catch her hand with rough, calloused fingers. "Mayve wanted you to know that. You still have me until Old Ced and his boy come back."

"I have no one." Vynasha snatched her hand free and gathered her cloak over her chest. She turned her back on the man Mayve had raised and saw the sack waiting near the back door. She'd crossed the room before Stye could catch her.

"Beauty!" Stye called after she had broken through the door into the back alley.

Vynasha clutched the sack close to her chest and walked as quickly as the icy rain and her limp would allow. It was better this way, better for Stye, if they kept far away. Let the villagers hiss and mock her. Let them buy her roses and pray they never knew their source.

In hindsight, leaving as she had might not have been her most brilliant moment.

For though she had claimed her precious supplies, not all feared her enough to stay away.

"Where you going with that, witch?" a gravelly voice called.

"Perhaps she'd like an escort," another chuckled.

Vynasha didn't dare look the rogues in the eye as she passed them on her way to the main street.

"What's the matter, witch? We not pretty enough for you?" Gravelly Voice said.

The men followed her, and Vynasha bit her tongue as her leg gave in the mud.

"Nasty witch!" the other man hissed. "Spreading curses in our village. Why couldn't you die with the rest of your cursed family? Always put on airs, they did."

"Enough," Gravelly Voice interrupted. "Take the bag."

Vynasha swallowed blood as she tried to run.

"Out o' the way!" A ramshackle cart suddenly barreled toward them.

Vynasha clutched her bag as she tried to jump, but the mud held fast to her ankle.

The men following her shouted as the cart narrowly avoided Vynasha and seemed to aim straight for them.

Vynasha turned to watch, her heart in her throat, and shivered against the rain.

The street had emptied. Would they have simply watched those men steal Vynasha's hard-earned goods? Was there no justice left in a world that preyed on the weak?

Her vision blurred, and her breath rattled in her chest as she battled her trembling. Hadn't Mother warned her they needed to be extra careful because they held gifts others feared?

Vynasha turned to the road home and froze.

A hunched and hooded beggar stood in her path, close enough to touch. Her skin prickled as he spoke. "You must take care of the road, Beauty. I shan't always be here to save you."

Familiar fury warred with the overwhelming curiosity she felt. "Who are you?"

The beggar stepped aside and lifted a bandaged hand to the road north. "Come, and I shall walk you home."

CHAPTER FOUR

A Life for a Life

THUNDER RUMBLED WITHIN smoke-wrought clouds as distant rain fell over the forbidden Wylder Mountains. A winter wind stirred a fresh wave of leaves from the nearby forest to cross their path. An odd scent lingered upon the air, wild and old, its hoarse moaning terrifying. Far worse than the voice Vynasha had been ignoring these past seasons. The voice remained silent as she kept a steady pace with the beggar who'd claimed to save her. If Vynasha weren't who she was, she'd think him mad. Had she not felt the prickling of something *other* the moment she'd laid eyes on him?

The beggar was dressed in a strange patchwork of garments that served as the cloak and hood of his robes. The hood was hollowed and deep, and strips of cloth had been wrapped tightly about the beggar's hands. A rotten stench accompanied the man, but fear and compassion kept her stomach from cringing in discomfort.

The hill on the northern path that would take her home often gave her leg trouble. This beggar moved just as awkwardly as she did during their brief climb. It was a strange comfort.

Silence accompanied them as they walked together, the beggar seeming more focused on sure footing than conversation, yet her curiosity grew until she pressed for answers. "You claim you saved me back in the village. How?"

The beggar didn't reply, yet she sensed a smile. Was he a foreigner? If so, what foreigner could possibly come from the forbidden northern mountains?

"Do you live around here?" She attempted a different approach. "I thought I knew all the families who farmed north of Whistleande village."

The road faded, splitting off to farms either abandoned or barely thriving. What families dared to remain lived in better circumstances than the once-overflowing village. The beggar did not venture down any of the paths she expected him to. Trees grew taller and closer to the path the farther north they climbed up the slope, along the edge of the valley. It would not be much longer before the only road left to turn down would be her own.

"You live alone, now, Beauty?" The beggar's raspy voice startled her.

"*Please* do not call me Beauty." Vynasha clenched her fists over her heavy wares and forced her feet to keep moving.

When the man spoke again, she could almost taste his sorrow. "Beauty such as yours should not live alone."

"Life doesn't grant favors to anyone, no matter how beautiful or ugly they are. Now, enough riddles. How do you know me? And don't lie. I'll know if you're lying."

The beggar turned his head slightly toward her. "Would you? Would you believe me if I told you I had met your kin before?" he whispered in a thin, papery voice.

She hated the desperate hope his words gave her. "Where did you see them? When?" The arm beneath her hands flinched, and

Vynasha belatedly realized she had grabbed the poor man in a too-tight grasp. "Forgive me, I just… please tell me what you know."

The beggar ran a bandaged hand over the rags covering his arm and hunched even further. "A man and his son were traveling west before they became lost on the road through the Wylder Mountains."

All feeling left her legs, and she barely caught her fall on the man's shoulder. "That's impossible," she hissed as she stumbled back from the beggar. "No one goes into those mountains because no one ever returns."

"I helped them find the path, on one condition," the beggar wryly said.

Vynasha dared close the distance between them. She doubted there was any disease this poor man had that she couldn't heal. Any risk was worth learning about Ceddrych and her father's fate. "Please tell me what happened. When my brother never wrote, I knew something must have happened." Rain stung her cheeks as she waited for his reply.

"The Wylder Mountains are cursed, Beauty," the beggar said with a harsh rasp, "and your kin could not leave of their own free will. I promised to find you, to tell you they yet live."

Vynasha turned back to the distant snow-capped peaks and felt the same powerful pull, the urge to follow that pull to wherever Ceddrych might be. But she had been disappointed so many times, and she was not strong enough to survive more. "I want to believe you…"

"Believe this, then." The beggar's bandaged hand entered her vision, a single blue rose in his palm. It was the rose she'd given Ceddrych in her hope it might protect him.

Vynasha sank to her knees as she accepted the rose. The petals were warm against her fingers, and she turned her smile to the beggar's shadowed face. "Please, tell me where he is."

The beggar buried his hands in the wide sleeves of his patched coat. "Would you choose to do what few have dared, Beauty? Would you brave the road through the mountains?"

Vynasha laughed. "Do I have a choice? If there is even a chance, I need to try."

"Fate can be a cruel mistress, and you will not find them as easily as you expect. If you are lucky, the man and his son will find you before the terrors do."

"My fate should have been to die here, like the rest of my family." Vynasha climbed to her feet and hefted her damp sack as though it could help ward off the hunger stirring deep in her empty heart. "I don't care how dangerous the road is or if I never come back. I'm going to find my brother no matter what it takes."

The beggar leaned back, and she couldn't tell for certain, but she could *feel* his smile and hear it in his broken voice. "A life for a life, then… very well." The beggar sighed as he lifted an arm to point to the storm-racked mountain range ahead, a land wrought by fear and legend. "Between the tallest peaks of the Wylder Mountains, you shall find a city. Should your kin not find you first, go to the city for refuge, but do not stop until you enter the castle. There, may you find the means to make your own fate, Beauty."

She frowned. In all the legends Ceddrych read to her, she had never heard of a forgotten city in the mountains. Then again, their library had been small, and no one ventured north anymore. "No one takes the old road. What if I lose the path the same way my father did?"

"Think of the lost city, and you will remain on the old north road, through many bounds and turns. Never stray to the east or west, and never try to come back."

Vynasha took several steps forward, giving in to the call of the mountains. Smoke from their cottage was dwarfed by evergreens. She could barely see the road continue through the thick forest that consumed it. Yet the longer she looked, the farther she could somehow see. "Would you come along? I'd feel better having someone along who knows the way."

"Would that I could, little starling, but this path is yours alone to take." The rasp of his voice faded in her ears, and she blinked as though waking from a dream.

With a sigh, she glanced back over her shoulder. "At least stay for—"

She froze.

The beggar was not waiting behind her, nor had he turned to hobble his way back south toward the village. He had vanished. The forest watching from either side of the road and the sloping, leaf-drenched plain was eerily silent.

And she was alone.

CHAPTER FIVE

A Journey to Be Made

SHE CAME HOME to a room masked in shadows and cursed the mad beggar for making her late.

Light from the dying fire near her bed cast eerie patterns over the wooden walls and simple furnishings. She didn't notice the silence until after she stoked the embers to flame under fresh logs. The absence of Wyll's rattling breath terrified her. She stumbled over her sack of goods on her way to the bed.

His skin was much too cold, and her heart ached to feel the misshapen flesh where the fire had been cruelest. She drew back the fur covers and pulled him into her arms. "Wyll!" She choked on his name, the most precious name left to her, the only one that mattered. "Sweetling, wake up, please…"

For several unbearable seconds, she felt no movement in his thin limbs, and it wasn't until her tears bled onto his neck that she felt him breathe against her ear. "Asha?"

Her gasp was both a sob and a laugh. She squeezed him tight, savoring the contact, willing him back to life. His hand rose to tangle in her hair, and she laughed again. "Wyll…"

"Don't cry, Asha," he said, so softly she almost didn't hear.

Unbidden, she thought of the beggar, of his taunting words and the illusion of recovering her brother in the northern wastes. It was a ridiculous enough idea that she would never have thought twice before Wyll's illness, only added it to the bedside tales her brother Ceddrych had whispered to her in the night. And yet she couldn't ignore the wild hope the beggar's words gave.

"*All legends stem from a certain truth, Ash,*" Ceddrych had often said. And what if he was right? What else besides Father's ancestral home lay forgotten in the mountains? What if she was killing little Wyll by keeping him cooped up here, surrounded by the memory of death?

Something snapped inside her at his sniffles, at the way his small hand squeezed hers, as though he wanted to reassure her all would be well. She and Ceddrych might never see the old ruins, slay a troll, or face a live dragon. But she could do this for Wyll. If this were to be his last winter, she would chase a fool's hope for the chance to reunite with what remained of their family. If she lost Wyll, then she would have nothing else to live for, anyway.

"Come, let's get some food in your belly," she said as she wiped her tears away.

Wyll smiled and nodded.

She spent the next few minutes helping her nephew eat and change into fresh clothes. He was still small enough to wear his old clothes, with a few additions made by her atrocious stitching. Being the youngest, she'd often shirked the feminine arts in favor of tending Mother's roses or running through the forest with Ceddrych.

But thinking of the ones they had lost would not make the journey ahead easier. No doubt her brother would have been horrified at the thought of her wandering into those mountains without him to protect her.

After she tucked her nephew into bed, Vynasha smoothed his brow with a cool rag, and for a moment, against the firelight, his eyes looked fresher than they had of late.

"Wyll," she began, "I've… heard word of your grandfather and Uncle Ceddrych."

"You have? Are they coming home?"

Vynasha pushed aside her fears and forced a smile. "With winter coming, they thought it better if we came to them. But of course, that will depend on whether you'd like for us to take a little adventure. It would be just like the old stories your mother read to you."

Wyll sat back against his pillow and sighed. "You can't mean a real adventure, Asha."

"I most certainly do," she retorted. "Cousin Stye will be so jealous when I write to tell him of our plans."

Wyll twisted the quilt and stared off into the hearth. A part of her ached to see the doubt and hope in his face. A child his age shouldn't worry as her little Wyll did. Even during the days when his heart was strongest and he was able to do light chores about the house, he never played. Since the fire that had scarred him so badly, he rarely smiled, and the sight made her want to see it as often as she could.

She took his hand in hers, bringing his gaze to meet hers. "I promise, Wyll. Tomorrow, we start preparations. We'll travel along the northern road, into the Wylder Mountains."

"The Wylder Mountains?" he whispered with wonder and more than a little fear. "Why would Uncle Ceddrych and Grandfather be there? You said only monsters live in those mountains."

"Those were just stories, Wyll. There aren't any monsters left in the world, only wolves and bears. Grandfather and Uncle Ceddrych wouldn't have made the journey if it weren't safe," she said with a brittle smile. It pained her to lie, but was it truly a lie? No one had been north in so many years. Who was to say what was true and what was legend?

Vynasha tangled her fingers together with her nephew's and squeezed reassuringly. "We've been through so much this past year, but winter is upon us, and I only wanted…" She shook her head before her desperation bled too much into her voice.

What if we don't survive the winter?

Vynasha drew in a calming breath. "I can't promise you the journey will be easy, but…"

"Asha," Wyll interrupted, "you kept me safe from the village when the others threw rocks at me. You didn't send me away when Grandmother Mayve wanted me." He frowned as he faced the fire again. "Sometimes, I wish the fire had swallowed me up too. Sometimes, I wish you hadn't saved me."

His chin trembled, and his gaze hardened. "But Mama would have wanted you to keep me alive. That's why we have to do this, Aunty Asha. Because she would want us to go to Uncle Ceddrych if we could. If you say there aren't monsters anymore, then I believe you. I won't be afraid."

Vynasha wrapped her arms around him and drew her nephew close before he could see her tears. "I should have known you'd understand, my brave boy."

This wasn't the first time she had awakened to tears and sweat. Her lips parted as she let out a shuddering breath into the cool dusk and wrapped her thin arms over her chest.

After gathering her robe over her bony frame, she pulled her waist-length braid over her shoulder and squeezed the dark curls left to fly free at its end. Moonlight shone through the curtain and played upon her skin. Winter's chill was settling over the valley, yet she could still hear the screams and feel the heat of the flames on her skin.

Ceddrych haunted her mind far more thoroughly than a pocket full of memories could. Over the past seasons, she'd often wondered if he was still trading with Father in the West. In her darker moments, she feared him dead and buried on some forgotten road. Vynasha didn't dare think about what would have pushed them to the Wylder Road.

Turning back to the dying flames, she placed another log upon the embers, and sparks danced up the stone chimney. The flames hurt her eyes and brought her no comfort. Instead, she turned reluctantly to the wooden chest resting at the foot of her bed and the small figure sleeping fitfully beneath the covers.

She unlocked the time-worn chest and let her eyes fall to the bundle of letters tied together. Her fingertips grazed the rough grain of old parchment, and it was her brother's laughing eyes she saw as she picked up the papers.

They had exchanged letters throughout the war with the Southern kingdoms. He had barely been home six months before Old Ced insisted on taking Ceddrych away from her once more.

As she glanced through the rest of the chest's humble contents—old tomes and faded finery—she realized they would need to leave most of it behind.

Vynasha swallowed past the lump in her throat and shut the trunk lid.

With unsteady hands, Vynasha lit a candle and began to read one of Ceddrych's many letters.

Ash,

Tomorrow, we leave for our first battle, and I don't think I could fall asleep even if I tried. I almost didn't write this letter, but I've written to you after our few petty skirmishes, and I know you would wring the truth out of me one day if I weren't completely honest with you. You've always seen right through me, little sister.

Because I cannot bring myself to lie to you, I won't pretend

I'm not scared. I won't tell you that because I've fought and killed men before, I'm not absolutely terrified for tomorrow.

I don't want you to be afraid for me, Ash. I'm not afraid of dying, not really. What terrifies me isn't eternal sleep but the possibility of never seeing you again.

From the moment I met you, I swore to Wynyth I would protect you. I think she knew even then the others couldn't or wouldn't. I think she saw how much I already loved you.

I'm going to fight tomorrow because I love you. I will do unspeakable, damnable things because I made your mother a promise. I will come home because I also made a promise to you. I fight not for fortune or glory but to keep our home safe. I will always fight for you.

Love,
Ceddrych

She read his letters until the wick burned out and fell into dreamless sleep.

At first light, Vynasha began preparing for their long journey. Thanks to her recent visit to the village, they would have enough to get by for at least a week. She pulled root vegetables from their meager garden to store what they might need later. After their supplies ran out, it would be up to the skills her mother and Ceddrych had taught her to keep them alive in the Wylder Mountains.

Vynasha spent the rest of the day preparing her neglected bow and arrows then beginning work on Wyll's sled. There were enough unfinished pieces Ceddrych had left in their barn for Vynasha to repurpose for their journey. She reinforced what she could with long limbs from younger saplings in the forest and twisted pieces of leather. Wyll laughed when he first sat inside to test her creation. As she worked, she prayed Dragos would be able to pull it most of the way.

By the time she deemed the sled strong enough, the sun was setting. Despite Wyll's protests, he saw wisdom in waiting another dawn before departure. That night, they slept together peacefully, with hope.

The following morning, Wyll said, "I dreamed I fought a wolf, Asha."

"Who won?"

"I did, but the wolf killed me too. Asha, what will we do if we're hunted by wolves?"

"I'd kill any wolf that came near you and skin it myself," she promised with a kiss to his scarred cheek.

Wyll's scars made his smile appear more like a grimace. "I wish we had furs to wear for when the first snow comes," he said as Vynasha helped layer her nephew in old finery.

She had already donned layers that would hopefully keep out the worst of the cold. "Where we're going, there will be plenty of game." Or so she hoped. Her skill with the bow had waned considerably since the fire.

Autumn's first snow arrived as Vynasha nailed her letter to Stye on the front door before locking the barn and turning to face the ruined ashes of what had been their cottage home.

She closed her eyes and clenched her hand around Ceddrych's blue rose. The scent of ashes was never far from her nose, even now.

Vynasha barely glanced at the rose garden as she reached Dragos, checking over the harness she'd fashioned to pull Wyll's sled.

"Are we ready?" Her nephew bounced with excitement from his seat.

Vynasha managed to smile as she came to pull the quilt and horse blanket more snugly over his slight frame. "Think the villagers will miss us?"

Wyll snorted as he batted her fluttering hand away. "Probably throw a feast with what's left of our harvest."

"How long before they break the lock on the barn door, you think?" Vynasha mused as she stood with barely a wince.

"Two days!" Wyll called after her as Vynasha rubbed Dragos's neck.

"Three, out of respect for Stye," Vynasha replied.

"Maybe they'll be too scared you left a curse on our land," Wyll teased, his one good eye gleaming brightly.

She pressed a kiss to Dragos's nose and whispered, "We have a long road ahead of us, boy." More softly, she added, "I can't do this without you. Otherwise, I'd never dream of taking you somewhere so dangerous. But I promise, I'll do everything I can to protect you so long as you help me protect Wyll."

Dragos nickered as he chewed on her braid affectionately then lifted his head from her shoulder.

Vynasha's smile faded as she looked past Dragos and Wyll to the smokestacks rising from the village far below. "Let's go."

The song Wynyth once taught her began with a low, soothing hum, perfect for beasts and journeys. Dragos followed her without a lead, and Wyll's sled moved easily over the fine layer of snow-covered grass behind them.

Wyll picked up the tune as well as his broken voice could manage as they passed the rose garden and approached the high tree line and clouds covering the northern peaks of the Wylder Mountains.

The old north road had not been regularly traveled since before Vynasha's father's family came to ruin, long before her birth. The faded ruts of carriage wheels of old remained, enough for Vynasha to follow as she left the last vestiges of childhood behind.

I'll fight you. I'll keep Wyll alive, and I will find you, Ced. I promise.

CHAPTER SIX

A Song of Winter

"*DO YOU COME at last?*" The voice in the wind came to her through the tall trees as Vynasha and Dragos walked through the day, snow filling the passage into the wild mountain range the higher they climbed.

With Wyll so near, she didn't dare answer as she sometimes did.

"*Come quickly, and be safe,*" the voice said, a soft caress against her ear. Vynasha shivered and pushed her stray curls aside along with her madness.

Once the sun reached its peak overhead, Vynasha paused long enough to slip Dragos's feeding bag over his head and aid Wyll out of his seat.

"It's so quiet here," her nephew said after relieving himself in the nearby trees. "Have you noticed?"

Vynasha passed him a small portion of dried and cured meat. "It's not exactly loud back home, either."

Wyll shook his head and nudged her side. "No, this is different,

Asha. Don't you feel it?"

Vynasha swallowed her bite with a grimace and a careful glance at the trees.

"It's just because we're in the forest," she said. She couldn't tell him that the same creeping feeling had bothered her ever since she stopped humming Mother's traveling song.

She had spent much time in the sparse wood near their old cottage and often heard other beasts wandering among the trees.

This forest was *too* quiet.

"Let's get back on the road," Vynasha said to Wyll as she led him back to the sled.

"Can't I walk for a bit, Aunty?"

She swallowed back her frustration and forced a smile as she squeezed his hand at her elbow. "All right. Just for a little bit."

Wyll helped her put away Dragos's feeding bag then kept a hand on Vynasha's arm as they continued up the narrow road.

The fire had damaged Vynasha's leg in a way that made it difficult to walk great distances. Wyll's scarring was far worse, and he tired more quickly.

They hummed the traveling song together, and Dragos pulled the lighter sled obediently.

Vynasha wished she didn't feel as though the forest was watching them closely. The beggar's words echoed in her head as she wove her mother's subtle magick.

"Think of the lost city, and you will remain on the old north road, through many bounds and turns. Never stray to the east or west, and never try to come back."

The winds brought flurries that swirled and ceased as the sun set below them. They walked until Wyll began sagging against her and her leg ached with sharp pain.

Before it became too much, Vynasha led them to rest on the path, confident no one else would be coming or going along this route. Wyll helped her to unpack their pallet and set up the tarp that would serve as their makeshift tent once they unhitched Dragos. Together, they made silent camp amid the grass and snow.

Over the following days, they fell into a routine. Vynasha barely thought to eat, only to make certain Wyll was provided for. Water was boiled from the ample supply of snow and stored for the following day's journey, though it barely seemed enough. Sleep escaped her when the weather nearly froze her limbs, but she found comfort that her heat was enough to let her nephew find peace in the night. Dragos rested, a steady sentinel at their backs.

Think of the lost city.

While Wyll slept, Vynasha played over the beggar's words and, when she did snatch slivers of sleep, awoke thinking of them still.

I'm coming, Ceddrych, no matter how long it takes.

Suns and moons rose and fell. Wyll had good and bad days but seemed happier than she'd seen since the fire. Some nights she read, from the one storybook she'd dared bring on the journey. Other nights, she read from Ceddrych's letters to give them both comfort. She left out or skipped the harder parts, when her brother had been worn by war and sorrow.

She grew blisters on her feet, and Wyll helped her apply the same healing poultice they used for his limbs to keep away bedsores. And the cold, at least, gave equal parts pain and relief for their mutual aches.

"How much longer?" Wyll asked on the fourth day of ceaseless travel, his good eye fever bright.

Vynasha smiled with what she hoped was confidence and replied, "Not long now."

"*Think of the lost city,*" the voice in the wind urged.

As the trees thickened and the mountains grew taller around

them, conversation stilted during the day. Vynasha often hummed her mother's songs to break the heavy silence. She kept a wary gaze on the shadows, wary of the beggar's warning. There were too many stories of travelers venturing this way, never to return.

Never try to come back.

Snow swirled before her eyes, often blurring her vision, and then suddenly, the way became so clear that she was captivated by the clawing, finger-like branches and the fragile beauty of the frost. She did not turn to look back for fear the old beggar's words would come true and they would be swallowed into the wood like those who had trespassed before. Every day, she felt watchful eyes on her drawing closer, and the wind whispered to her of something forgotten and primal, now trapped in the spirit of these mountains.

"Do you feel like we're being watched?" Wyll asked one distant night by a fire as they ate the meager bits of dwindling supplies.

"Maybe…" Vynasha hedged. She had led them a bit off the path to camp by a nearby stream. Dragos seemed grateful to draw from a direct source rather than munch on the frigid snow. The river drew her to their campsite, and it was easily within sight of the old road. The sound of the rushing water was comforting.

"If it was wolves, we would have heard them, wouldn't we?" Wyll asked.

"Yes," she agreed. "Try not to worry, sweetling. We haven't seen much on the road, but maybe that's a good thing. Fewer predators."

Wyll tossed pebbles in the rushing stream, and the smile on his face pushed aside the ache in Vynasha's heart. She would need to hunt soon. They were out of meat, and the rest wouldn't last beyond another week if she gave most of her rations to Wyll.

They needed fresh hide as well. The extra cloth she had wrapped around her feet inside her father's old boots did little to keep the snow from seeping in… or stop her blisters from breaking afresh. She was making plans and wondering how to keep him safe while she left for more supplies when Wyll cut through the silence.

"Asha, I've never seen these stars before. Have you?"

She couldn't help smiling at the way he craned his neck to see past the smoke and spark of the fire. "Strange, but you're right." She frowned and rubbed her layered arms.

"Did you know it's been ten days since we left?" He pressed his lips together and smoothed the better half of his face from expression. "The trees are bigger, and the air tastes funny here. But I feel stronger too." He smiled faintly. "Maybe tomorrow, I'll walk part of the road with you."

Vynasha nodded and bit the edge of her thumb. "Maybe, sweetling."

He *had* seemed better the last day or two. While he tended to run short of breath, he had lasted longer yesterday.

"We're almost there, Wyll. Only a few more days before we meet Uncle Ceddrych," Vynasha promised.

Please, she prayed to the stars, to whoever was listening, *please.*

They both savored the fresh water they drank from the clear riverbed and fell asleep together, listening to the sound of the stream. Vynasha hid her tears in Wyll's hair and prayed she was not leading them to their deaths.

She dreamed she was swimming with Ceddrych in the Southern Sea he'd described in his letters. "*Water so clear you can see straight to the bottom, Ash.*" He'd promised to take her there one day, "*after the damned war is over and I can steal you away for a real adventure.*"

They never made the journey, and she'd never learned to swim.

Which was why Vynasha woke with a jolt and clawing panic to feel frigid water pulling her hair downstream.

The river.

Vynasha sat up with a shout and grasped at the rocky riverbed.

She had fallen asleep tucked against Wyll, so why was she waking up in a river?

Flowing water rushed over her bare, scarred hands. It should have been freezing, even with her loss of feeling since the fire. Instead, the water felt almost comforting.

Her breath came faster as she jerked her hands from the riverbed and twisted around to take in their surroundings. Her hair and part of her clothes were soaked through from what should have been an icy grave, but it wasn't until that moment she felt her blood freeze.

Wyll and Dragos were missing.

All the peace she felt moments ago vanished as she called, "Wyll!"

The forest was silent and far too still.

Her throat closed even as she struggled to call her nephew's name again.

A boot splashed into the stream beside her, and a shadowed figure bent to lift her from the water.

"Let me go!" she growled as she kicked and fought against the man carrying her out of the river. She cursed the fact she'd left her good knife in her pack as she fought harder then screamed, "Wyll!"

"Easy, girl. You will be well soon as we get you before a warm fire." The man's deep, rasping voice blew over her face.

She scrunched up her nose at the mixture of pipe smoke and dead animal that clung to her would-be savior. "I don't know who the hell you are," she hissed, "but if you don't tell me what happened to my nephew and my horse, I swear on my mother's grave I'll—"

"Relax, little witch! You will find me far less harmless than the likes of this evil wood. The steed and your boy are safe, I promise you." He lifted his bearded chin to a path he seemed to know well.

It was difficult to make much out of their surroundings in this stranger's arms but especially with the world bathed in a fresh veil of snow. Best for now to see if this stranger would stay true to his word. Should he turn foul, Vynasha doubted she could run far. Her body had mostly healed in the year since the fire, yet she would need greater strength to survive on her own. If anything happened to Wyll, she would lose any reason to go on. And the stranger's constant mutterings were not easing her discomfort.

"Foolish children must have been wandering for half a moon. A wonder the wolves did not snatch them first."

Vynasha did not want to know more about the wolves he spoke of. She was mistrusting of strangers but especially ones who appeared in the middle of the Wylder Mountains.

Against her will, the man's warmth made her limbs relax, and her lids shut of their own accord.

CHAPTER SEVEN

A Foolish Man

VYNASHA BLINKED RAPIDLY against the bitter winds beating against her face, her mind dragged back by the hunger in her belly and the pain in her limbs.

You can't be in pain if you're dead.

Sound and scent came next: the pop of burning wood and ashes.

Flames dripped from the walls in hideous curls.

She opened her eyes with a gasp and turned to face not the raging inferno of her dreams but a campfire spilling light over the nearby trees. Something shifted against her chest, and she pushed aside the bundle of furs to reveal Wyll, fast asleep beside her. Her hand trembled as it came to rest over his steadily rising and falling chest.

Tears blurred her vision as she lifted her gaze to the other side of the campfire to find the grizzly man who had rescued them. The stranger dug his teeth into the roasted leg of some dead creature and spoke while he chewed.

"She wakens at last, Resha. Did I not tell you she was real?" He pointed the meat toward Vynasha. "Mayhap I was right, and another has come at last? Like a lamb led to slaughter, more than a curse breaker, I think. What say you, daughter?"

Behind them, tied to a nearby tree, Dragos nickered at them, clouds of hot breath spilling into the air from his nose. No one else sat around their campsite, though it was hard to make out much past the fire's glow with the trees packed tightly around them.

Vynasha frowned as she spoke clearly as her damaged throat allowed. "I'm not your daughter."

The man laughed so hard in response his beard bristled and his brows quivered. Wyll stirred in his sleep against her chest.

"No, you most certainly are not my spawn, child. Resha, come out of the shadows. The steed is calm, and you can see they are no threat."

Vynasha jumped when the shadows beyond the firelight shifted and a brown face framed by bright amber eyes appeared.

"Do not worry, girl," their savior chuckled. "My Resha does not bite unless I tell her to."

As Resha crept closer, Vynasha could see it was black furs and not shadows that encompassed the mountain man's daughter. The young woman might have been Vynasha's age, but her eyes seemed far older, and there was little kindness in her expression as she crouched before the fire.

"She cannot speak, my Resha. Daughter, show our guest what mark the wolves left you."

The young woman pushed back her hood, revealing tangled black hair. When she began to untie the lace at the top of her tunic, the firelight gleamed against a necklace of ragged, teeth-like scar tissue which ran from her chin past her collarbone.

Vynasha's hand found her chest, where the worst of her scars lay hidden. Resha's hard gaze followed Vynasha's hand before shifting up to the burns that disfigured her face and softened.

You understand, the young woman's grim expression seemed to say.

"Beast nearly ripped her throat out, but you showed 'em the old rip and curl with your blade, did you not?" The man chuckled and tossed the rest of the roast to his daughter. Resha placed the wolf's-head hood of her cloak back over her head and tore eagerly into her father's scraps. "Aye, that pelt she cut from the wolf that savaged her. I taught my girl well, did I not?"

Wyll had dreamed of wolves. And these people, the only people they had seen since entering the Wylder Mountains, lived where worse than wolves were said to roam. These people were neither beast nor wolf, yet Vynasha sensed the same danger from them all the same.

"Who are you?" she asked.

Wyll stirred in her arms again. This time, his good eye stared wide and wary of the strangers in their midst.

"I am called Wolfsbane. My daughter and I are the last remnant of the old mountain folk. You children come from the flatlands, then?"

Snow drifted onto her nose, and across the fire, Wolfsbane watched for her reply.

"No, we came from Whistleande, in the valley to the south."

"So there is life south of our cursed borderlands. Did I not tell you, Resha?"

Resha scowled at her father before cutting her wide eyes to Vynasha then Wyll, and something like compassion softened the amber edges.

Wyll squirmed again.

"It has been many moons since anyone has seen strangers come from the flatlands," Wolfsbane said as he motioned to his daughter. "Well, feed them, girl! Look at the poor lambs, half starved already," he mused.

Vynasha accepted the bundle Resha left inches from her reach. The meat she found within was rarer than she might have preferred a season before. Now she ate it just as eagerly as Wolfsbane's daughter had, passing the most tender bits to Wyll. And while they ate, the man told Vynasha what she already knew.

"These mountains do not want visitors, and I should warn you, there is a great darkness that holds these lands. But if you hunt with us and earn your share, I will let you stay. The boy is clearly too weak to care for himself, but we can put him to good use still. Better to wander with us than take a chance out there."

Vynasha licked her lips and tucked what she could not stomach into the inner pouch of her cloak. There would be time to eat later. And as tempting as Wolfsbane's words were, she couldn't forget the true reason they'd come. "I appreciate your offer. But we didn't come here to learn to hunt. We're looking for someone."

"Ah, so it is like that, then…" Wolfsbane smiled, revealing chipped and stained teeth as he nodded to Resha. "I was right, pup. This one was called here." To Vynasha, he said, "Whoever you think to find here, whatever evil spirit sent you on your journey, you would do best to return to your flatlands and your Whistleande."

"I can't go back," she said. "I was told to find a city in these mountains, that my brother is there. Besides, even if we wanted to, there's nothing waiting for us where we came."

A wolf cried in the distance, and Dragos shifted closer with a nervous rumble.

Vynasha reached a hand behind until she could reach the horse's flank. "Steady, boy," she whispered.

For a long moment, Wolfsbane studied her. Resha pulled free a wicked-looking blade from her cloak and had turned to watch the tree line. Other wolves echoed the cry of its brother.

Vynasha kept a firm hand against Dragos's flank as he strained against the lead. Wyll shifted back against Vynasha until she'd tucked him tightly beneath her arm.

"Many of our people went to this city you speak of for favors or answers to their woes," Wolfsbane finally said. "None returned. Many moons ago, I met a man who passed through this territory, same as you lambs, a desperate man willing to make a foolish bargain. We never saw him after he left our company in search of the lost city. I warned this man he walked to his death, but he didn't listen."

"He's *not* dead," Vynasha growled, chest heaving as she swallowed. "I'd know it if he was dead."

"Mayhap not," Wolfsbane replied, pity in his wild eyes. "But if you should seek those same gates, know there is truth to every legend, little witch. Great evil slumbers in that city and has been dormant for an age. Pray the one you seek did not waken it."

There's a reason no one ever goes north. A reason men cross themselves when the Wylder Road is mentioned.

Vynasha did not want to think about the possibility that Ceddrych had been that foolish man any more than she wanted to lead her nephew into a lost, wicked city. Wyll's hand found hers as she whispered, "Can you show me the way?"

A strange smile lifted the corner of his mouth. "Oh, it often finds your kind first. But I can guide you part of the way. You have a greater chance of finding what you are looking for if you will trust your instincts, little girl."

The wolves' song had long since faded, yet Resha continued to prowl about the edges of the tiny clearing. Wolfsbane's eyes followed her passing with a weary smile. "My Resha is all I have left in this world, along with the hunt. We survive because we trust our instincts, and because when the call came, I bound her until the urge to follow passed."

Vynasha stiffened as Wolfsbane's hard gaze settled over Wyll.

"If you are going to the lost city, you know you must leave the boy behind with us."

"Asha, no!" Wyll cried out, begging with his one good eye. "I'm not afraid! I can keep up, I promise."

Wolfsbane held her in his unrelenting gaze, and her heart tightened in her chest as she spoke without meeting Wyll's eye. "If he came with me, he'd die." She knew the truth before Wolfsbane confirmed her fear with a firm nod. Even Resha returned to the fireside, her brow furrowed as she crouched closer to them.

"I'm not afraid of dying!" Wyll argued, his breathing labored. "I feel stronger since we came here, remember?"

Wolfsbane chuckled. "You feel magick at work in you, boy. But your body is not strong enough for this journey. Not with wolves and worse about. My Resha will watch over you."

Resha startled at this, glaring at her father even as Vynasha tried to settle Wyll's continued protests with hushed whispers. Dragos whickered softly behind them.

"Asha, please don't leave me alone. You promised…"

She wiped the tears from his good eye. "I won't be gone long, just to meet Uncle Ceddrych, and then I *swear* we'll come back to you."

"We have a hidden place where they can stay until your return," Wolfsbane said to Vynasha. "I will keep a close watch on the border of the lost city for the first week. If you do not return by then, trust that we will guard and keep your Wyll safe."

Wyll muffled his tears in her chest, his hand snaking around her back in a desperate grip.

Vynasha's lips trembled, but her words were firm. "We have an accord."

Leaving Wyll had never been part of the bargain. But she didn't know what she would be facing in this lost city. She couldn't carry Wyll on her back if she were forced to run, and by the look on the wild man's face, trouble was certain to find her.

Wolfsbane laughed. "After all I've said, you must truly be mad, girl. But we will help you both as I've promised. Too few people remain in our mountains. We must band together, or we will fall, same as the others did. Tonight, you must sleep and rest, knowing Resha and I will guard your sleep. We will never be farther than a scream away, shall we, daughter?"

With those words, the beastly man turned his back to them to begin his watch, and his daughter Resha slipped back into the inky night.

In the quiet that followed, Vynasha held Wyll and whispered, "It's going to be all right, sweetling, you'll see. You heard the wolves earlier, didn't you? You saw Resha's scars. We both know I'm not strong enough to protect you alone. Wolfsbane's right. If there's even a chance I don't come back, I want to know you're not just safe. These people aren't like the villagers. They're different, like us. They'll teach you how to survive…"

A small hand came to rest on her face, forcing her to look at him, and she was startled at the depth of knowing in his tear-stained face. "Who will keep you safe, Aunty Asha?"

Vynasha held Wyll closely. "No more tears. It's like you said, Wyll. I kept us alive before, and I'll never stop until I find Uncle Ceddrych. Besides, there is magick in this land, in the trees and in the water. The magick will make you stronger until I come back. Maybe then you'll walk the whole way with us to find our new home. Maybe you'll even run."

She opened her eyes to find her face numb and her body half buried in a fresh drift of morning snow. Inside Wolfsbane's furs, however, she clung to the remnants of lingering body heat and the comfort of her nephew's breathing. Vynasha tried to memorize the smell of him and the way every breath was a struggle. He was so smart, like Tamyra, so clever his mother would have been proud of him. More than any of her family, Wyll deserved to live a long and happy life.

The campfire was blackened, and snow-covered coals mixed with smoldering ash. Besides the furs covering them and the satchel placed at their feet, the rest of Wolfsbane and Resha's belongings were packed and secured on their owners' backs. The odd duo communicated in hushed tones and gestures near the ruined fire.

"You understand what's at stake, daughter. The wolves must never find you or the boy. I will cover our territory for now. Leave the hunt to me."

Resha hung her head a moment before nodding resolutely.

Vynasha jumped as the young woman suddenly turned to meet her eye.

"Ah, she wakens at last!" Wolfsbane greeted her with his arms outspread.

"Asha?" Wyll stirred against her arms, and Vynasha's grasp tightened. She couldn't shake the irrational fear that this would be the last time she held him.

"The sun shall soon rise," Wolfsbane said, "and the time has come for us to part ways. Ready, pup?"

Resha nodded to him before hesitantly approaching their pallet.

Vynasha blinked against the sudden sting in her eyes, unable to release Wyll from her fierce hold.

"Let me go, Aunty," he whispered as he pried her hand from his chest. His image blurred against the weight of her tears.

She blinked and nodded, pushing his hair out of his eyes. "Listen to Resha and Wolfsbane while I'm gone. They… they'll keep you safe."

He nodded, a flicker of fear reflected in his pale-blue eyes. His arms wrapped briefly around her neck. He hugged her the same way he had after the fire, after the fevers had subsided and he'd become aware enough to understand what had just happened. Her tears spilled down her cheeks as she hugged him back.

It was over too soon. Resha helped Wyll to stand and, keeping an arm secure under both of his, helped him walk to the mended sled.

"Aren't you taking Dragos?" Vynasha asked as she sat up.

"Too dangerous for such a beast in this forest," Wolfsbane cautioned.

"I thought you said the lost city was worse," Vynasha deadpanned.

Wolfsbane chuckled as he turned to Resha. "Be careful of those tracks, daughter. It'll be harder to throw the beasts off."

His daughter gave him a tight nod and shared one last look with Vynasha as though to say, "*I swear I'll keep him safe.*"

Vynasha stood, pulling the furs over her shoulders with her as she tangled her fingers in Dragos's mane and watched as Resha slowly pulled Wyll into the pale emptiness.

Dragos nickered and nosed her chest, startling her attention from the forest's shadows, from the lingering tracks Wyll's sled left behind. She pressed her palm over the burlap satchel and the pocket containing Ceddrych's letters. Her breath filled the air like an opaque cloud of smoke, and she closed her eyes, seeking the gut feeling the hunter had spoken of. Nothing but emptiness answered. The only thing she could do now was to move forward.

"Are you ready, little witch?" Wolfsbane broke her concentration.

It took little time to ready her pack. She had run out of extra grain for Dragos just before their failed camp beside the river. But he had already foraged amidst the snow for any lingering grasses and shrubs nearby. She could only pray it would be enough.

Just a little bit farther, she thought as she ran soothing hands over his flank and settled her pack over his back. She secured the bow and quiver to the saddle beside her satchel.

Wolfsbane waited patiently, always keeping an eye on the trees, until she led Dragos to his side, nodded, and took her first steps into the silent wood after him.

CHAPTER EIGHT

A Lost City

UNLIKE THE NIGHT before, Wolfsbane kept quiet on their steady climb from the forest camp. She grew accustomed to the steady crunch of their steps and decided she preferred the silence to more of his terrible tales. She'd learned enough to be wary, and even Dragos seemed to share in the careful silence. Sound echoed in a forest but was usually broken by other creatures in the wood. Or so it had been in Whistleande Valley.

Nothing about Wylderland made sense to Vynasha. Not the preternatural silence and lack of fowl or game, not the almost constant howl of wolves somewhere in the distance. Certainly not the way a familiar voice carried along with the icy winds.

"You will be safe soon. Not much farther. I will guard your path."

Vynasha shivered beneath her furs and gritted her teeth before Wolfsbane could hear them chatter. She was suddenly grateful Resha hadn't taken Dragos, grateful to have one last piece of her family at her side.

She had often heard the voice in the wind, sometimes with Wyll at her side in the rose garden or near the village. She glanced over to find Wolfsbane's head on a constant swivel. The mountain man was nearly as tall as Dragos, and with all his trappings again appeared more bear than man. And he seemed oblivious to the voice and her fears.

He led her back to the path they had strayed from, though she didn't remember it being lined with silver cobblestones before. Perhaps Wolfsbane's camp had been farther north? Vynasha stared in wonder and resisted the urge to touch the glittering stone. But surely, as the mountain man had claimed, something must have wanted her to find the lost city. She forged ahead to the sounds of her worn boots and Dragos's hooves clinking over the metal path.

Lost in thought and memory, she startled at Wolfsbane's thick hand on her shoulder. "Here is where I must leave you, little witch. I will follow so long as I'm able. But the rest of the journey you must make alone."

"How long?" Her voice wavered on a rasp as she clutched Dragos's mane.

"Long enough to rip into any beasties that may seek to eat you." He chuckled, yet his smirk faded as he added, "Your scent is known to us, and we shall not mistake it. And if you are lucky, if you are strong enough to face the wickedness and win, we shall meet again."

Vynasha caught his weathered hand in a fierce grip before he could pull away. "Please look after my nephew. He's only had me for so long, but he trusts both of you. He's very weak, more than he will admit, and the cold only makes it worse…"

Wolfsbane squeezed back. "My daughter and I are the last of the old mountain folk. We have our own magick for keeping the boy strong and safe."

"Thank you for everything." She might be a fool for trusting

Wyll's life to strangers. But did she have a better choice? At least this way, whether she found Ceddrych or death, Wyll had a chance.

With a heavy sigh, she turned back to the cobblestoned road. Wolfsbane faded into the nearby forest, a silent shadow she still sensed but couldn't see.

"*Better the beast you know,*" Mother used to say. She kept this in mind as she pushed her feet forward and kept her eye on the silver road.

Gooseflesh prickled at her skin as a sharp wind carried the sudden cries of wolves. Vynasha picked up her pace, and Dragos seemed eager to follow.

"Better the beast you know," she whispered with a careful comb over his mane.

When the high snowbanks receded and a carpet of blue grass stood in its place, disquiet crept back into her soul. The greater forest gave way, and slender silver birches lined the metal street. Though a layer of frost and ice laced every surface, the air didn't feel as crisp as it had before. It felt like the roses she called when no flowers should bloom. It tasted of magick.

Vynasha paused and glanced over her shoulder. Sure enough, tall snowbound fir trees stood like a wall behind. The forest had changed faces with less than half a league of travel. The howling of wolves sounded far in the distance, but it was difficult to judge. And a familiar voice whispered to her in the wind, "*Not much farther now.*"

Everything here seemed perfect, and the lack of color made the blue grass startlingly bold. She tensed as her feet found more stone than earth, the path gradually emerging the farther she walked.

No more flurries descended over these high, winding mountains, and the frosted berries she found along the road and meat Wolfsbane had given her filled her stomach as they walked. Dragos munched heartily on the blue grass. She no longer sensed her silent protector nearby.

"He can't go past the boundary," she muttered to Dragos. Mother had spoken sparingly of magick. Most of what Vynasha knew came from watching her tend the roses or creating small potions to heal minor wounds and ills. But in Wynyth's songs, there was more. And in Ceddrych's legends, magick users had been capable of deeds both great and terrible.

Shadows filled the cobblestoned path until she couldn't see through the waning daylight. Heavy footsteps echoed in the wood behind, the first she'd heard since entering the Wylder Mountains. Soon, the few became many. Was this the evil Wolfsbane had spoken of?

She ignored the aches in her feet and bad leg and urged Dragos to pick up the pace. She didn't have the heart to ask the poor beast to carry her on his back. Dragos was just as weakened as she, judging from his prominent ribs.

Cracks and steady thuds echoed in the silver birch forest around them. Her heart raced as she ran a hand over the bow tied to the saddle, and her free hand fell to the rusted blade at her hip. Why hadn't she thought to trade for a better knife before leaving Whistleande?

A cold, sickening fear coursed beneath her skin as she urged the old horse to move faster. Dragos shifted nervously, a steady wall of warm flesh at her side. She refused to turn back now.

Shadows drew in together, obscuring her way until Vynasha could not see the silver trail. She couldn't outrun the darkness, and the steps behind her quickened to match her pace, accompanied by low-pitched growls.

A year ago, she might have risked facing the threat with her bow, when she still had the strength and agility needed to fight.

Tears blurred her vision as she turned to Dragos and whispered, "I'm sorry," before throwing her good leg over his back beside her pack and clinging to his neck.

Dragos groaned yet did not hesitate when she begged him, "Run!"

Vynasha's heart seized in her chest as Dragos burst forward in a surprising surge of strength. The last of the sun disappeared behind the mountains as they pushed blindly into the blackness. Her heart raced in time with each snap at Dragos's hooves.

Tears streamed down her cheeks. She might never find the lost city or Ceddrych. She might never see Wyll again. Despair morphed into fury, and she buried her face in Dragos's mane and tightened her legs' grip along his flanks. Her flesh burned in the cold and with the same fury that gave her strength the night of the fire.

"*Hurry! Don't let them catch you,*" the voice in the wind urged.

"Help us!" Vynasha cried back.

A yelp echoed through the wood, followed by a snarl of a beast far larger than whatever snapped at their heels. Vynasha dared peer over her shoulder to see thin and tall shadows overwhelmed by a creature far larger.

She bit back a scream and faced forward as Dragos's hooves clopped against stone once more. Sounds of a vicious battle fell distant, as they were once more guided by the silhouettes of trees and the road. And a looming wall just ahead.

"Slow!" she cried as a thick mist shrouded them.

Dragos struggled to ease his pace with a pitched scream.

The wall bore holes, scrolling vines and metalwork, the same as the road.

Vynasha clenched her teeth as she flung her hand out. Her hand pressed against air yet felt as though it slammed into the metal of an impossibly high, wrought-iron gate.

The gate gave way just before Dragos crashed into it, allotting just enough space for them to squeeze through.

Immediately after, the gate snapped shut with the grate of metal on metal.

Dragos trotted ahead through the mist up the twilit silver path. Vynasha's chest heaved, and she pressed her lips to her horse's mane with a whispered, "Thank you."

She wasn't sure if she was grateful to only Dragos or both him and the monster that had saved them. Dragos's sides heaved with haggard bellows, reminding Vynasha they were already pushed beyond their limits.

"Stop. I can walk now," she beckoned, though her leg ached terribly.

The old horse simply whinnied at her in reply and continued at a slow trot.

"Stubborn." Vynasha chuffed and pushed herself to sit atop her friend's back.

Her eyes widened as moonlight spread over the valley they came to between the mountains.

No longer bound by snow, the land ahead was made of soft blue grass and hills which gleamed silver in the night. They were so high now that clouds hugged the snow-capped peaks around the narrow valley, and everywhere, a low-hanging mist glistened as though lit by tiny gossamer pixies. The scent of magick was stronger past the gate.

The road widened as they trod close to the crux of the valley and the nearing mountains and, built along both sides, strange stone buildings. No candle or firelights within, no lamps. Nothing but darkness and death.

The road led right into the lost city, and Dragos did not stop. Not as Vynasha dared to peer into the gaping windows and shiver from the sense they were being swatched. Nothing living lingered here, this she knew for certain. She was suddenly grateful Dragos had insisted on carrying her. Would the ghosts of this city stay within their stone tombs if he hadn't?

She kept watch on the lost city as the road became a long

stone bridge, unable to shake the feeling pricking at the back of her neck. That if she took her eyes from the city for one moment…

Dragos nearly unseated her as he came to a sudden halt.

Vynasha cursed as she struggled to find her seat, only to gasp as she looked up and still higher up. The road had ended, cut off by the highest wall she had ever seen. No, not a wall… a castle.

Dragos shifted uneasily on his hooves, and Vynasha did her best to comfort him. "Easy, boy." She groaned as she slowly dismounted, keeping one hand on Dragos to keep her footing.

The wall was so sheer she could only see the shadow of the silvery night above. Before them, square-cut stones outlined a door that stood higher than the highest rooftop in Whistleande. Even as her hand met the images engraved in its massive handles, she could not believe her senses.

Vynasha barely touched the monolithic door before the colossal wood gave way and the wind whispered, "*Welcome home.*"

After all they had left behind, Vynasha refused to leave Dragos outside in the cold. Surely, there would be a stable of some kind, even if she found no one living within.

Ceddrych is here. I know he's alive. I would know if he wasn't.

Yet as she tried to lead Dragos behind her into the shadowed entry, her horse took two steps back.

"Come on." Vynasha grabbed his lead and grunted as she tugged against his impossible weight.

Dragos reared his head, and the whites of his eyes showed as he refused to enter past the shadows of the castle.

Vynasha cursed and pulled again, only to jump back as Dragos snapped at his lead with his teeth. "Stop it! I'm not leaving you out here, you stupid oaf!"

Dragos tossed his head and then stepped forward to press Vynasha toward the entrance with his nose.

She gasped and clung to him, pressing her forehead to his

nose. "I can't go on without you."

Dragos whickered low at her but would not respond to her pleas.

Vynasha's teeth dug into her lower lip as she removed the lead and makeshift harness. The pack was harder to unseat when all her limbs shook with effort. She wasn't even twenty years old yet, but she wasn't strong like she had been before the fire.

She refused to cry as she shouldered her pack, then her bow and quiver, and told her only remaining friend, "I'll find a stable for you, but if it's too dangerous and you can't stay… go back to the blue grass field. Go where it's *safe*, and I'll find you."

Dragos nipped gently at her curls as she slipped an arm around his neck and breathed in his scent. Her horse shifted, dislodging her arm, before stepping back and pressing her forward with his nose again. *Go on*, he seemed to tell her with solemn dark eyes.

Vynasha turned and did not look back as she crossed the threshold. The door closed with a gentle yet heavy thud behind her.

She hesitated as soon as she saw the slush she had already tracked in. Her battered and cracked boots were far too filthy to walk on such a rich surface. She shivered as she hobbled over a floor of mosaic glass. The strange silvery metal she had followed into this lost kingdom now stretched out between cracks far into the candlelit distance. Her fingers loosened as a rush of shock and disbelief assaulted her.

Someone must live here after all.

Vynasha wasn't sure if that was a good or dangerous thing.

As she took in the breadth and height of the castle, she felt the weight of unseen eyes, as though something was waiting to see what choice she made next.

Lofty shadows kept her from making out the chasm above. Balconies overlooked the entrance of the grand hall, where candles winked and danced from their perches. A wide staircase wound its way higher to hidden floors. Pillars braced the weight of the staircase and rafters several paces ahead. Hundreds of candles, which lined a crimson carpet, sat upon silver candelabras.

Every step was now agony. Vynasha pushed aside her pain and followed the halo of flickering candles past the entrance hall and into a smaller passage.

Tapestries covered the walls on either side of her path, and exhaustion must have been the reason the strange beings and images shifted the longer she stared. Vynasha gasped and dug her nails into her palms to quell her anxiety.

Deep alcoves broke the walls, guarded by grotesque statues of creatures in pain. The crimson carpet split off into other doorways, some filled with darkness and others masked by heavy wooden doors. Despite the sea of candles, proof that *someone* must dwell here, she could not vanquish the sense that told her this was a tomb.

Tears spilled over her cheeks, but she couldn't give up, not until she'd followed every last candle. Not until she knew for certain Ceddrych was not here. No matter what Wolfsbane had said, no matter the beggar's promises. No matter if she was doomed to wander this ruin for ages without success until she, too, gave in to stone and collected dust. She walked blindly, aching for the warm fire she remembered from their cottage.

The sudden roar of flame and illumination ahead startled her. *Magick.*

Old magick, by the taste of it, like the crushing layers of fallen petals in Wynyth's garden. As she stumbled down a set of carpeted steps, Vynasha realized the entire castle reeked of enchantment. Not benign magick, either, but something wicked and cruel.

The room she found herself in was illuminated by a hearth higher than her head. The flames were large enough that they might have threatened her nerves were she less exhausted. Now, the promise of warmth after endless days of sleeping in the elements was inviting enough that she sank upon the rug. Her tangled mass of locks tumbled free from her loosened braid over her shoulders as she pried off her shawl.

Vynasha pulled her wet fingerless gloves free and set them beside her shawl before lifting scarred hands to warm before the fire. Her scarred flesh took longer to warm, and she struggled to feel it, numb from the damage she welcomed to save Wyll's life.

The night you failed to save anyone else.

What would she tell Ceddrych if she found him in this dark place?

"Please, forgive me," she whispered, biting her bruised lip as the urge to lie down and sleep in this bitter tomb overwhelmed her. "I'm not strong enough, Ced. I'm just not strong like you…" She curled into herself as she rested her head on her damp arm. She needed to remove her sodden layers, wrap up in the rug if nothing better presented itself. But she was so tired, and what magick Mother had passed on to her wasn't enough to fight her failing body. If the cold didn't stop her heart, then this starvation certainly would. Her one comfort was that little Wyll was with Resha and Wolfsbane now. They would care for him, keep him safe from the things she could not.

"Just sleep for a little while, then search the rest of the castle," she whispered to the flames. If she did what Wolfsbane deemed impossible, if she survived whatever evil slumbered in this place, she *would* make a better life for them after this. She stared into the fire until the weight in her eyes became too great.

The cloying stench of old magick seemed to clear as her eyelids slid shut. A new scent permeated the room, overpowering the taste of ashes on her tongue. The evergreen forest after a winter storm, the land cleansed in a blanket of death.

"Beauty?" It was the voice in the wind.

Strong hands lifted her, tilting the world on its axis as she was cradled closer to this scent and a soft-as-down fur cloak. "Hold on to me, Beauty," the voice beckoned, deep and rumbling against her ear.

Vynasha turned into the heat and clean scent of the forest, free from old magick. Her hands were too weak to find purchase in the fur cloak. Threads slipped through her fingers, yet she clung on as best she could and whimpered, "So tired…"

"You need not be weary anymore, Beauty. Never again," the voice replied.

She floated for a time, and the voice hummed a soothing song in deep bass. Vynasha tried to hum along, as the tune was familiar, like something she'd heard in a dream long ago.

The gentle rock as the voice carried her higher and still higher lulled her into a perfect, dreamless sleep.

CHAPTER NINE

A Waking Dream

"WYLL.... DRAGOS..." SHE needed to find her way back to them. Was Wyll safe? "Dragos too cold," she muttered as she fought against an invisible weight that was keeping her limbs down.

Wake up. You need to wake up!

She couldn't open her eyes, and though her limbs twitched, she felt removed from her body.

Am I ill?

The voice in the wind spoke to her, closer and more present than ever before. "You are safe, Vynasha. No one will harm you here."

"My horse?"

A warm hand, strangely soft and sharp at once, grazed her brow. "Already resting in our stable."

Vynasha's limbs settled. She shouldn't trust the voice so easily. But the voice had urged her to run back to the house a year before. Wyll was still alive because of the voice.

The voice began to hum once more, a slightly strained medley she almost remembered. Images from her youth danced behind her eyes as the world spun and turned. The click of a door latch interrupted the song. Past the memories, flashes of pale silvery light broke through the darkness.

"Speak if you must, Odym, for I have little patience," the voice nearly growled.

"Forgive me, Master, but you asked for my report once Grolthox returned to the castle." The intruder's voice was odd, as though she were listening to him speak through a veil of ice.

"He should not have been able to leave the grounds at all," the voice grunted, though the hand gently caressed her brow once more, pushing aside her hair.

The intruder sighed before answering. "He is less bound than the others in his beastly form. And a part of him will always be aware of her. It could cause problems."

"You *will* tell Grendel to keep his pet in line, old man. This maiden is our last hope."

A ringing in her ears drowned the rest of their words out, no matter how she fought to keep aware.

Time slipped through the cracks, and she fell deeper into the tide of her dreams of Ceddrych's gold and green-flecked eyes. Of Tamyra's gentle fingers carding her tousled locks and Mother singing in the garden.

Until the dreams twisted into Ceddrych, wounded and dying alone in a distant land. Of Tamyra's screams and little Wyll's freshly scarred features illuminated in a cast of wildfire.

Vynasha reached blindly for something to pull her from the flames before they consumed her too. "No!" She gasped for fresh air.

"You are safe, Beauty." A deep voice rumbled against her ear. The forest and freshly fallen snow filled her senses as her fist closed over a handful of fur, and with desperation rather than strength, she drew it closer. "Please," she begged, needing more.

The voice drew in a sharp intake of breath before carefully lifting her up. Vynasha sighed in winter's embrace.

"Sleep and forget…" His words calmed her enough to sink into sleep and find a pocket of peace. In her dreams, she was in the forest once more, frozen rigid in a mountain of snow, the rush of a babbling brook ringing in her ears, and she drank from the waters before darkness clouded her mind.

She blinked her eyes open to a single beam of golden light and lingered between sleep and wakefulness. The crackle of a nearby hearth and the utter stillness of her dark surroundings confused her. Had the beast been nothing but a dream? Her stiff limbs tensed with the strain of wasted muscles. Her fists clenched over the warm folds of her bedsheets.

Vynasha dragged the sheets up to her face and inhaled the scent of foreign spices and snow. With a gasp, she sat up and found herself at the center of the largest bed she had seen. Heavy velvet curtains hung from a canopy, obscuring her view save a tiny sliver of firelight. Her heart pounded in her chest as she leaned forward, but she could see little past the nearby hearth. She crawled to the end of her bed, trying to ignore the dull throb in her bad leg, and pushed the curtains aside.

How did I get here?

The glow of candles and hearth fire illuminated the room. Set within prongs attached to the wall, each candelabra held three of the same sticks she had seen on the landing. Tapestries cloaked the walls, only these were covered with images of rose gardens and a maiden with her back turned. Thankfully, these did not whisper to her as the others had.

As she stood, she realized that someone had undressed and

washed her as well. Her feet were bandaged and covered in stockings and slippers. She ran clean fingers over the red silk dress she had been changed into in wonder and mild frustration. Never had she worn so fine a dress or shoes so rich and soft. And not since she was a child had anyone dressed her without her permission.

The beast was part of my dream… wasn't it?

Vynasha wrapped her arms around her chest as she took to examining each piece of furniture, from the dresser drawers to the bookshelf tucked in the corner and the table at the opposite end. Nowhere did she find the ratty clothing she'd arrived in or her old pack. It was the sack's contents above all else that pushed her to look harder.

A tall wardrobe claimed much of the space beside her canopied bed. She cringed when she met her reflection in the long mirror inside the door. She still looked like the monster the children of the village feared.

Her black hair hung down her back in heavy curls and partially masked the mottled scars which hugged the side of her cheek and spread down her neck. Kisses from the fire that killed her family. After so many days in Wylderland, any excess flesh had shed from her cheeks, leaving them gaunt and her gray eyes set deep within her ruined face. She placed a scarred hand over her reflection.

She pulled, and the doors opened with a creak, revealing a plethora of robes and dresses. Rich fabrics and jewels glinted in the candlelight. Who had cleaned and undressed her? Again, she thought of the scars running down her body and shuddered to think of what they had seen. With a bitter twist of her mouth, she shut the wardrobe door and turned her back on her reflection.

The howl of the wind called from a floor-length window. Pushing the heavy drapes aside, she pressed her fingers against the frost-laced surface and peered down. Lofty mountains plummeted into an abyss below. Somewhere out there, her nephew lived on the hospitality and protection of strangers.

She turned her head at the knock on her bedroom door. Eager and dreading to meet her jailor, she hesitated only a moment before clenching her jaw and hobbling across the thick carpet. Twisting the door handle, Vynasha pulled the heavy wood, and gears creaked as it opened easily.

A silver tray waited in the hall before her feet. Beyond the candelabras on either side of her doorframe, nothing but blackness revealed itself. Chills laced her spine as she thought she caught a flash of glowing silver from the shadows before it winked out of existence.

A small part of her longed to flee, but the darkness brought on memories of the beast. She hated herself for being a coward, yet something inside warned what would happen should she dare the empty hall. For all she knew, whoever had brought the tray waiting at her feet could still be watching.

Play their game for now. Learn what you can. This place is clearly not as abandoned as you thought.

A single scroll of parchment rested on the silver tray. Vynasha braced herself on the doorframe as she bent to retrieve the scroll. The silver had been polished till her wary reflection peeked back at her. The parchment was heavy, and the wax seal bore a coat of arms she did not recognize. She hated to break it at first, wary of what she would find inside.

Play their game. If there are people here, Ceddrych could be here, too.

The script was heavily penned with black ink in letters that crawled across the page in an archaic fashion. Only the elders in her village were familiar with the old language, since their laws had been written in it. But thanks to Ceddrych's rare collection of books, she knew enough to grasp the meaning.

"*Sequere candelas,*" she read aloud, rubbing a finger over the ink. "Follow the candles?"

The candles flickered as a fresh draft of wind and whispering voices graced her ears. She shivered as she took a cautious step back into the safety of her room. Her fist closed over the parchment as she brought it to rest against her pounding heart.

Ornamental prongs hung along the wall leading into the dark hall. The only candlelight clung to either side of her doorway. Vynasha bit down on her cheek as she waited for the darkness to come to life.

"There is nothing there," she hissed. "Move." She tasted blood on her tongue as she crossed the threshold and stepped over the silver tray.

The unlit candles on the walls flushed to sudden, fierce luminosity. Vynasha covered her mouth with the back of her fist and stumbled on her bad leg. The parchment crinkled further as she tightened and loosened her grip. "Come on," she whispered as she followed the trail of candles down the long hall.

Her skirts swished, forming a small train behind her, and she took minimal comfort in the soft-toed slippers silencing her steps. Crimson carpets ran along the passage she followed from her room, marked by carved alcoves and gold-threaded tapestries. "*Too late… you can never escape now,*" they whispered as she passed other closed doors.

Vynasha cursed and forced her gaze forward, resisting the urge to look upon their enchantment. The taste of magick filled the air, warning she needed to keep her senses about her this time.

Am I the only prisoner in this hall?

As the path of the candles twisted and turned, the ceiling suddenly broke away to sudden heights. Chandeliers hung from impossibly high perches, watching over balconied halls that whispered of another level of the castle. What had Ceddrych thought of this place?

"*We could leave this valley, just the two of us, Ash,*" he'd once said. "*Trade old Dragos for a real horse and just follow the sunrise. Maybe we could even find out if the old kingdoms have changed.*"

"Stop it," she growled as her throat tightened. No use dwelling on the past if she were to stand before her captor and demand her belongings, her horse, and her life. Lifting her chin, she squared her shoulders and tucked the memory of Ceddrych and his promises deeply within.

The path ended at a tall, blackened door, which creaked as she pushed against it. She stumbled back when it swung the rest of the way on its own, revealing an enormous dining hall inside. Heads of beasts and skulls of legendary dragons were mounted on wooden posts high above. A banner marked with a much larger version of the coat of arms she had noticed in the scroll's wax seal hung over the great hearth. The tapestries in this hall were grander than those she had seen thus far and shimmered in the light of the flames.

With a jolt of recognition, she took in the hearth, the crimson carpet, and small stone steps leading down toward it from the other side of the room. Only the hearth had illuminated it on her arrival at the castle. Every candlestick in every corner was lit now, from the walls to the long wooden dining table sitting in the room's center.

That wasn't there before.

Vynasha willed new strength into her bad leg as she carefully took the few steps and entered the room with the soft swish of skirts. A dozen different aromas wafted from the bowls and plates waiting at the head of the table. She tried not to be intimidated by the tall chair she sank into.

The hot meal was separated by so much silverware and glasses filled with different drinks that she scarcely knew where to begin. Her mouth watered as she took in the steam rising from some kind of glazed meat. With a quick glance for her absent host, Vynasha snatched a fork and tucked into the fresh food as quickly as she dared.

A low moan escaped her throat as her taste buds sang against her first hot meal in weeks. Her eyelashes fluttered as the candle flames wavered in a sudden draft. Slow, labored steps echoed in the dining hall, the heavy animal-like breath accompanied by the click of clawed feet muffled on carpeted stone.

Her fork clattered against her silver plate. The back of her neck froze against the sudden weight of eyes. Biting back a curse, Vynasha moved her hand to grasp a tall glass by its neck and began to drink the startlingly sweet liquid. When she shut her eyes, she could almost hear a voice say, *"You are safe, Beauty."*

Vynasha turned toward the hearth to greet a tall figure garbed in an indigo robe as it emerged from the shadows. The darkness he drew from clung to him still, masking his features as he greeted in a rumbling voice, "Enjoying your dinner, my lady?"

It was the beast from her dream.

The voice in the wind.

CHAPTER TEN

A Hope and a Bargain

"IT'S YOU," VYNASHA breathed, her grip painfully tight on the arms of her chair.

The beast shifted, a subtle tilt of a shadowed paw as he approached two chairs set before the great hearth. "Apologies for the meager fare, but we cannot afford better with the wolves attacking our borders constantly."

"Why are you not joining me?" Her voice creaked as she took in the shift of a tail beneath his sapphire cloak, the twitch of pointed, furred ears, the glint of horns.

His massive head shifted, revealing a sleek, black-nosed snout, casting his silvery fur with golden firelight. "As you might have guessed, it is not a simple matter for me to eat as you do. I would not wish to ruin your appetite."

Her meal forgotten, Vynasha gathered her skirts and crossed the hall to meet him. A wiser person would have stayed put. But the beast had not harmed her... yet. And Vynasha needed answers. The swish of her skirts met the beast's ears, and his silver fur bristled in the firelight.

"Are you so certain you wish to greet a monster, Beauty?" He sank against the wings of a high-backed chair.

Vynasha's fists clenched her skirts as she slowed her steps. "You don't seem like a monster to me," she whispered as she caught the jewel glimmer of his green eyes.

"You may feel differently one day," he replied, hand stretching out, black claws clicking together. "But if you insist, please. Have a seat, my lady."

"That depends." Vynasha ducked her head as she rounded the other high-backed chair and dared peek at the beast. Deeply set eyes burned into hers, set above a muzzled jaw, framed by golden horns which gleamed atop his head like a crown. He was greater in breadth and size than any beast or man yet seemed to be trapped somewhere in-between. Her breath caught in her throat, yet still, she asked, "Am I your prisoner?"

"Yes," he said with a grave rumble. But those too-intelligent, too-*human* eyes left her with the sense she was far more than a prisoner.

You should be terrified.

But she was too curious to be terrified just yet. No matter how impossible such a creature must be, her captor may be the only one that had the answers she sought. Vynasha worried her lip between her teeth as she dared to sit in the seat beside the beast. "For how long?"

The beast tilted his head slightly, lips curling back at the side to reveal sharp fangs. "That depends entirely upon you, Beauty."

Vynasha pushed her shoulders back and answered with more strength than she felt. "I suppose it was too much to hope for a forthright answer."

A low rumble answered her that she soon realized was a chuckle. "You may suppose, indeed. Unfortunately, I am as bound by enchantment as you in this cursed place. There is much I cannot tell you. But please ask, and I shall give what answers I can."

Holding his heavy stare was difficult. Vynasha couldn't remember the last time someone held her gaze without disgust or pity. She worked the soft fabric between her fingers and wondered again why she wasn't afraid. Certainly, this beast was dangerous. The promise of violence was writ in his claws and teeth, yet his eyes were almost kind. And he appeared to be as curious about her as she was about him.

"I heard your voice before." She paused to catch her breath, and his gaze sharpened. "I heard you call to me in the wind." She shook her head and ducked her chin. "I sound completely mad, I know."

A silver-furred hand, shaped like a man's, tipped with black claws, reached into the space between them, only to curl back again. "Why am I surprised you should ask the one thing I cannot say above all else?" The rumble behind his voice might have been another laugh if not for the strain in his voice.

Vynasha forgot her heated cheeks as she met his sad gaze. "I'm not a fool, you know. I know there's a heavy enchantment over this place. My mother could speak with her roses. I know a little about magick, and I know that you or this *place* called me here. I'd like to know why."

The beast nodded slowly as his gaze shifted to take her in before settling on her eyes. He didn't spare a second glance at her scars. "Magick has called you here, but forgive me. I cannot tell you why."

Vynasha sank into her chair with a sigh and managed, at last, to tear her gaze from the beast to the fire. "Mother told me stories about the rules of magick. You said this place is cursed, and the bindings on you must be strong. I just wish…"

"What do you wish, Beauty?" the Beast was quick to interject.

Vynasha grimaced. "That you'd stop calling me Beauty, to begin. My name is Vynasha, and it fits me far better than that silly nickname ever could."

The beast hummed deep in his throat. "Beauty is far more than flesh, Vynasha. I call you Beauty because you *are.*"

Vynasha pressed her lips together as the heat returned to her cheeks. She couldn't be sure if she was angry at his insistence or flattered. Yet if he knew who she really was and what she had done, he wouldn't find her so deserving.

"And if there are to be introductions," he continued with the hint of a smile, "I suppose you may call me Ferox, or Beast, as you prefer."

Her cheek strained from the smile she hadn't noticed she returned.

Fool. Are you trying to frighten or befriend him?

Vynasha ducked her head, aware her smiles were no pretty thing. "Beast, I heard that others have come here before. Are they… A young man came through these lands. Perhaps he is still a guest?"

The beast was silent for a moment. "Many have come to our realm in search of an answer to their woes," he began. "Most perish before reaching our gates. You are fortunate to have reached our doors unscathed, Beauty."

"Oh," she whispered, squeezing her eyes shut before the tears could escape. Her nails dug painfully into her palms.

He's not dead. You would have felt it.

Candlelight shivered between them as the wind kicked up and then settled back with a hush.

"Beauty?" Ferox's voice drew closer. "I am sorry I do not have the answers you seek. What I can offer you, however, is the chance to rest and recover from your journey." His green eyes glowed with compassion and an unspoken plea.

She clenched the fabric of her skirts even tighter. "What do you propose?"

"Remain here in this castle as my guest willingly, and I will see to your every need," he began.

"My horse, Dragos?" she interrupted. "I won't leave him in the cold so close to whatever haunts your lands."

Ferox inclined his head. "Your friend is already a guest in our stables and quite content, as my servants last reported."

Vynasha bit back a smile. "And my bow, my pack? There are things inside I'd like returned to me."

At this, Ferox grimaced. "I am sorry, my lady, but you were discovered half dead before this hearth with nothing but the ruined clothes upon your back."

Ceddrych's letters…

Vynasha slumped into her chair and swallowed back fresh tears.

No more tears.

"What else?" she asked, with a strength she didn't feel. "What's in it for you?"

"Besides the pleasure of your company? You shall dine with me here each night, but I must request, for your safety, that unless you have an escort, you remain locked in your room."

Vynasha's muscles ached with fresh tension and the crackle of magick beneath her skin. "Can you tell me why?"

Ferox shook his head slowly, an unspoken apology in his emerald eyes. "This castle is not a safe place after moonrise. Even I do not wander while the mad beasts roam the castle."

"What if I refuse? What if I take my horse and leave tonight?" Not that she had any intention of wandering alone in these black, enchanted halls. Not that her body was fit to carry her anywhere without provisions.

All humor and kindness fled Ferox's beastly visage. "Then you will indeed find yourself locked inside a prison of your own making, Beauty."

CHAPTER ELEVEN

A Dark Enchantment

WHEN VYNASHA OPENED her eyes, it was to silence and a crick in her neck. In her dream, the shadows beyond the castle walls haunted her, prowling outside her room, raking their claws against the door.

She pushed herself up with a groan and tried to ignore her aching leg as she slipped her feet into a pair of soft slippers. She closed her robe over her nightgown and padded over to her window.

A blizzard raged outside her prison, masking all but an endless abyss beyond the stone ledge. Vynasha saw herself in that pit, trapped by Ferox and her bleak future. Resting her forehead on the pane, she took in an unsteady breath and froze when she heard sibilant voices in the wind.

"Come and see. See what has been hidden…"

She had spent so long hearing Ferox's voice in her head, but something about these unfamiliar voices set her nerves aflame. The scent of magick thickened, and a chill trickled down her spine as she glanced over to the tapestry on her wall of the maiden among roses. Vynasha blinked and left her vigil by the window.

The girl in the tapestry had shifted to glance over her shoulder at Vynasha.

The voices grew louder, whispers layered upon whispers, neither masculine nor feminine.

"Come and look, follow… this way, quickly! Before they see."

Vynasha dug her nails into her calloused palms and glared at the tapestry as the maiden continued to stare back at her with a coy glance. "Stupid to listen to anything in this cursed place," she muttered.

But… well, she *was* curious. Enough to cross to the tapestry and follow the tang of magick until a faint draft met her fingertips.

The girl's eyes had followed her, and the maiden smiled with slightly sharp white teeth.

Vynasha grimaced as she pulled the tapestry aside and gaped at the small door behind it. "Right. Must be a servant's entrance."

The prince of Whistleande had lived in a house with servant's halls. Better to keep the help out of the way, so Tamyra once said. Her sister would know. She'd been forced to work there a whole season while her husband left for the wars to the south. Wyll hadn't been born.

The door behind the tapestry swung open, dragging Vynasha's thoughts to the present with a start. The passageway beyond was dimly lit, and the walls were covered in faded carvings. Her slippers whispered against the dusty stone floor as she dragged a hand over images of winged people and monsters with horns.

Just like Ferox.

The door clicked shut behind Vynasha, and she cursed as the wood refused to budge against her fists. There was no door handle.

"Stupid," she hissed as she pressed her back to the door. The hall stretched far into the distance on either side, the floor a dusty gleaming silver, same as the path that had led her to the castle. "Only one way to go, now."

Drawing her robe more securely over her chest, Vynasha followed the carvings and the growing hum of magick thrumming in the air. Cobwebs clung to the hidden corners of the walls and dripping ceiling. Vynasha ignored the occasional scuttling of vermin and the flashes of silver light that always seemed just beyond her vision.

The passage twisted and turned, shadowed doors appearing often on either side. No doorhandles on these doors, either, though an echo of sorrow lingered in the walls.

Until she reached the end of the dusty passage, faced with a door framed by golden light.

Vynasha caught her breath as she pressed her hands to the door, and it gave way easily. A new passage, illuminated by torches set in strange prongs carved to resemble tree limbs, sprouted from the walls. These flames burned so brightly, the silver floor reflected their warm glow. What stole her breath away were the brightly painted frescoes she slowly walked past. Much like the carvings from the other passage, the frescoes depicted people who seemed made of the forest mingling with others who wore fur instead of skin at festivals and tournaments.

She watched with bated breath, but the whispers didn't return, nor did the paintings come to life. Instead, this new passage echoed with the distant roaring of beasts, something neither bear nor wolf.

"*Even I do not wander while the mad beasts roam the castle,*" Ferox had said.

The path declined then turned in a slow arc before stopping before a carved door far grander than anything she'd seen so far. Strange to find something devoid of color in this brightly lit hall. A prickling sensation burned her hands as they hovered before the carving of a horrifying creature's face, its face permanently trapped in agony upon the blackened door.

Vynasha shook her head before she could lose her nerve as she pushed the door open and stepped into the vast room beyond.

The breadth of the room was slightly smaller than the dining hall in which she'd shared dinner with Ferox. No candles illuminated its corners. Moonlight from the balcony graced the obsidian pillared corners, the four-poster bed, the smashed, overturned mirrors, and wooden chests that rested against the walls. And at the center of the room, a strange arch stood, covered in silver runes and gleaming as though filled by a layer of glass.

"A mirror?" she whispered as she hobbled over to the source of power that she'd felt from her room.

A buzzing of magick and sudden whispers filled her senses as her steps came to a halt before the liquid shimmer.

"Yes! See? See what has been hidden? See what you must protect."

Vynasha's hand trembled as she dared to press it to the rune-carved arch. It was made of stone, but no stone she'd ever seen, and it was…

Warm?

Wind stirred from the nearby balcony and a single snowflake flew inside, gliding to the surface between her and the enchanted mirror.

"Careful, Curse Breaker," the voices hissed.

Vynasha jumped as she heard the sudden rush of heavy galloping steps. Cold terror gripped her chest as a great shadow fell over her.

A heavy paw hit her side with one powerful swipe. Its claws ripped through the fabric of her dress and past the flesh of her back as she was thrown up into the air. Her body collided into a bed. Her head cracked against a broken pillar, and she fell in a crumpled heap on the floor.

Ferox. The name came to her mind but couldn't pass her lips. Still, she struggled to pull herself onto her hands and knees, knowing she was about to die. Through the roars in her ears and the howls being carried by the wind, the creature's bellow pierced through the fog. Somehow, she found the strength to rise and turned to face the blur of dark fur bristling in the shadows.

This beast was as unlike Ferox as he to a wolf. Golden eyes glared at her from a creature that was a cross between a hulking brown bear and a lion, fangs drawing past its lower lips in a furious snarl. This must be one of the beasts Ferox had warned her about. But there was something else, something pained and almost *human* in its luminous gaze.

Vynasha spat blood as terror twisted into raging fury, her blood flushing hot in her veins. Magick dulled her senses. Or maybe it was the impact. She needed to fight back. She had so much more to lose now with Wyll waiting out there for her. And Ceddrych was still alive—she felt it in her bones.

Vynasha shifted on her bad leg, and the burning in her veins brought feeling to deadened nerves in her hands and face as she shouted, "GO AWAY!"

The beast snarled then roared as snow from beyond the balcony suddenly shot through the open door in a flurry.

Vynasha gasped as the snow continued to pour unnaturally through the door, pelting at the beast, stinging her exposed skin. Her vision blurred as the beast was forced back several steps, and the unnatural storm coated her in a sea of white.

Vynasha's bad leg gave out first, and she came to her knees with a painful thud. Tears of relief escaped her eyes as she sank to the floor. She turned her head from the bear-like beast as flashes of silvery light winked in and out of the storm.

"Wake up."

Vynasha woke with a scream on her lips, the nightmare of claws fresh in her mind.

A hard, icy hand smashed against her lips, and the voice from before hissed, "Quiet! Unless you wish to have every monster in this castle bearing down upon us."

Vynasha nodded as she waited for her eyes to adjust to the dim light. The stiff hand brushed across her lips, and flashes of silver light shifted, giving the shadows form. "Where are we?"

"Where do you think?" The silver shadow figure brightened to unveil a thin man kneeling before her, observing her with piercing, pale eyes. A faint beard shadowed the bottom half of his face and surrounded a mouth twisted in a wry curl. He gestured impatiently at the nearby wall sconce, and a small flame erupted with unnatural blue light.

"The dungeons," she muttered. "How did I…" The smell of damp decay clashed with the stranger's oddly familiar scent. She groaned as she focused on the tension in his shoulders, the badly hidden panic behind his fierce gaze. "Who are you?"

"Drink." He lifted a flask to her lips.

She hesitated, half expecting this to be another trick of the eyes.

"I am the gatekeeper of this prison," he grimly replied, "and you, unfortunately, were dragged here by one of my charges."

Vynasha narrowed her eyes as she tasted the water on the lip of the flask and barely bit back a groan. It tasted like *heaven*.

He grimaced when her fingers inadvertently lay over his. Had she not spent her life observing her own family and the unhinged state of her village in the years following the war, she might not have noticed. The anger he held at bay was barely concealed within his gaze.

"I'd give you my thanks, but your *charge* nearly killed me," she said after she had drunk her fill and pushed up from the filthy rags.

"Grolthox is harder to control than most." The gatekeeper drew back a safe distance as his gaze flickered to the dried blood darkening her torso. "How could you be so senseless as to wander these halls at night? Have you not been warned to keep to your room behind lock and key?"

Vynasha lifted her eyebrows. "Why didn't you keep your damned beast locked away like you were supposed to?"

He tilted his head, drawing her attention to his pointed ears and smoky gray skin. "Have you considered that I have already corrected my mistake and am attempting to rescue an ungrateful madwoman?"

"I'm not mad." Vynasha bared her teeth as she moved purposely into the flickering blue light. "What I am is cold, injured, and ready to go back to my rooms, *please*." Her fists ached with the sting of ice, skin that had not truly felt for months.

Rather than gasp at her scars as she expected, the gatekeeper's frown dug deeper into his face, and his eyes flashed with a curious violet glow. "As gaoler, it is my job to tend to the mad. Since you obviously have a death wish to have come to this cursed place, you should be aware. Not a single maiden who answered the call has ever escaped."

"Believe whatever you want about me." Vynasha gripped her knees tightly, pressed her lips together, then said, "I'm not here to claim a kingdom but to find my brother." She frowned, wondering at her own state of mind, at her desperation to believe the old one's words when he had been a stranger. Yet he must have saved her. Or she would be beast fodder by now, wouldn't she?

Though clearly discomfited, the gatekeeper extended a hand to help her stand. "Listen," he began and then hesitated as she met his gaze. "I cannot let you loose to go tromping around this castle at night. But I shall help you, long as it gets you out of my way." He bowed his head and rubbed his fingers over his fist. After sticking his head out the dungeon door, he shook his head and murmured to himself, "We will be lucky if the whole castle does not learn of this." He stopped short when she closed the space between them and wrapped her arms over her chest.

"You'll help me escape?" His gaze followed her movements as

she rubbed a hand over the claw marks in her corset.

"I am the gatekeeper, and I will keep you safe," he whispered without meeting her eye. The door opened of its own accord, and she eyed it warily.

They bypassed many other cells on their journey through the castle's underbelly. Water dripped from cracks in the low ceiling. It looked ancient, as though the mighty bricks that had formed the tunnel had had plenty of ages to grow black and coated with fungus, which had died, cracked, and then reformed once more. Pockets of yellow glowworms lived in corners, lending eerie luminosity. Occasionally, the brick gave way to the caves it had originally been carved from.

What frightened her most was not the atmosphere or the gatekeeper leading her by torchlight but the unearthly screams and moans. She fought a constant battle not to cover her ears with her hands, to block out sounds of agony that slipped through the locked cages. Her eyes fell to gaps, dreading yet needing to see what waited on the other side. The bars were of a metal she had never seen before, red-gold and glowing. Though she didn't find the burnt golden eyes of her beast, there were others. Too many. Once, she lingered too close to the bars, close enough for a claw to slip through and tear at the fabric of her dress.

"Grolthox!" the gatekeeper growled while pulling her to his side. He thrust his torch between the bars, and a snarl and whimper answered. The other beasts and captives howled and whimpered and rattled their trappings.

Vynasha gasped for breath and flinched when she recognized his grasp. His touch was like packed snow against her waist. It made her tremble because she was unused to being touched by anyone other than her nephew. She wanted to vomit because of the rush of her blood pooling beneath his touch and the sensations prickling all over her stomach.

He wasted no time in pulling her along after him until they had ascended a tower and entered the corridor above. Only then did he release her to take several steps ahead. Instead of leading on, he paused and slipped his torch into a nearby sconce. He pressed his hand against the wall and sank his weight against it as he hung his head.

Vynasha couldn't help but watch with curiosity. Perhaps it was because she had spent so little time in the company of people. Or perhaps it was this place, this fortress, slowly turning her mad against her will, that made him glow brighter before her eyes. Had he been Ceddrych or her nephew, Wyll, she might have wrapped her arms around his waist and begged him to confide in her.

His sharp tone cut through her budding sympathy. "Never wander the dungeons by yourself, Vynasha," he said, glancing back at her over his shoulder.

"How do you know my name?"

He released his grip on the stones. "I know what the walls whisper in the night. I know what Odym and the other servants say of you."

Odym... the name was familiar, like something she'd heard in a dream.

The gatekeeper tensed when she came up beside him. She frowned as she tried to piece her thoughts together. "Are you like them, then? Like Odym?"

To her surprise, he laughed, and when he turned to face her, his smile was bitter. "After all this time, I may as well be."

When he moved past the torchlight, she wondered whether they would be able to see the road ahead at all. She shivered at the thought of having to touch him again for guidance. Once the shadows had claimed him and she was forced to follow, a change took place. The instant the inky dark draped over him, he glowed like the others. He avoided her eye and instead took hold of her with a firm hand.

The rest of their journey up was made in silence—all the better, for she needed to think. She needed to forget the past events of the night. But she would have never left her cabin if she weren't prepared to face whatever dangers stood in the way. The world was more wondrously strange than she had imagined, and she had no intention of running from it now.

The castle looked different with the dawn creeping in. Occasionally, it cast the walls in various shades of marble and sparkling granite and worn tapestries like the pages of a book, so she might glimpse a reflection of their glory days.

So many questions were swimming about in her mind. Though she wanted to ask her guide, it was best to seem more ignorant than she truly was. As she had learned from her father and Adriaa and Iona, people rarely said what they meant or meant to reveal half of what they said. All would reveal itself in time.

This man had promised to help her, though he didn't know just how literally she had accepted it. She would not forget.

CHAPTER TWELVE

A Truth Most Inconvenient

VYNASHA HAD BARELY slipped back into her bedroom through the hidden passage when the doorknob rattled. She dove for her rumpled covers and desperately willed her heart to slow as the door creaked open.

Flashes of light passed behind her closed lids, and Vynasha feigned sleep as low whispers met her ears. "Another troubled night for the poor dear, looks like. Wonder if her nightmares are about whatever caused those awful scars?"

Vynasha flinched and hoped the servant didn't see. From what she could hear, there were two, and possibly female. Only one bothered to speak as they pulled a fresh dress free from the wardrobe and set it over the nearby chair.

"Wonder why he placed her here in the old mistress's rooms? I know *I* would have poor dreams if I were forced to dwell where *she* haunts."

Old mistress?

Vynasha wasn't surprised she wasn't the first, but she should have realized long before now where the fine clothes had come from.

What happened to the woman who came before?

"Well, let us hope Master asks her tonight and the new mistress accepts… we will not last much longer, that is certain."

Vynasha dug her nails into her scarred palm as the door slowly creaked closed. She peeked through narrowed eyelids to glimpse luminous figures slipping through the doorway before the door clicked shut.

Vynasha released a long, rattling breath through her pursed lips as she pushed her curls out of her face and stared at the canopy. "Well…" she muttered, "one thing's certain. I'm never going into that bloody passage again."

Vynasha shook her head as she climbed out of bed and skipped the steaming tray to remove last night's ruined clothes. She glanced at the newly roaring fire and considered the merits of shoving the clothes under the bed versus burning them. It would be such a shame to waste even filthy fabric. But she couldn't afford the maids to discover blood on her clothes, either.

"Last thing I need is Ferox asking questions," she whispered as she stripped and fed pieces into the flames. "Not like they have a shortage of dresses."

The wardrobe was fit to burst as it stood. As the undergarments smoked in the wide hearth, Vynasha opened the doors and grimaced as the full breadth of her scarring reflected at her from the mirror within.

She pulled on the drawers for fresh underthings to go along with the dress the maids had already laid out. The drawer stuck, and something rattled and bumped from within. Pausing to grab and don the first stays, shift, and stockings she could find, Vynasha slipped her arm back in and reached for the back. Her frown deepened as part of the drawer above came unhinged. Two objects dropped into her hand, and she pulled them free to inspect by the rekindled hearth.

A key unlike any she had seen before, made of white twigs twisted into patterns and yet hard as metal, rested atop a pale, leather-skinned book.

Moving to sit before the flames, she opened the nameless leather-bound cover and pored over the elegant silver-inked script. Much like Ferox's note, the words were written in the old tongue. Vynasha translated as best she could.

Once, I was known as Soraya, beautiful as the stars and terrible as Queen Haydra of the Fayere. Now I am nothing, reduced to this baneful existence, bound to these white walls as much as I was once free to fly on the night winds. He has reduced me to nothing with his cruelty, his indifference and hatred for my kind. How the sparks of evil were lit between our two peoples, not even I know-I who came to this mountain to undo his treachery and bring peace between our worlds. I have failed.

The king lies dying as I form this ink from scattered dust in the air. And I have not even torn down his wicked house as my mentor demanded. I have failed. For with his death, I will be bound to this prison forever, never to see my homeland again. To him I gave the chance of life upon a silver platter with myself as his consolation prize. One look upon the mask of beauty I wore and he was mine, until his greed for power consumed him. Soon, his son shall inflict an even greater reign of terror on the peoples than his father thought him capable of.

Yet I have remembered in the long hours of darkness, with moonlight and shadow as my companions, the old power that the old queen whispered to me with her dying breath. "Shattering evil and crumbling it to dust requires the greatest sacrifice."

It has already begun. My strength wanes with each passing moment. Soon, my spirit shall haunt the halls of this place until all fades and the balance is restored. If I am successful, not even the power of the gate will be enough to unlock this spell, and my vengeance shall be won in the end. Yet my heart grows heavy within me as my true love speaks to me. His eyes burn each time he passes me what sustenance is given to keep me alive. He has heaped the plate with his own portions. I beg him not to, yet he is of the wylderfolk and will do as he pleases. Should I be thankful he was the one ordered to guard my prison?

I tell him the old ways, resting against this door as he leans upon the other side. I can hear his heart beating and the smile in his voice. It is almost enough to know someone will mourn me. And a strange need compels me to write now. I mustn't allow the knowledge of the past age to fade with me. So I will tell it as it was once told to me, and as I saw with my own eyes, what happened so long ago.

Vynasha jumped at the sudden knock at her bedroom door and dropped the book and key on the rug at her feet. Cursing under her breath, she realized she hadn't finished dressing. Her eyes darted from the door to reach the woolen day dress. She was tired of so many mysteries with so few answers.

Deciding, Vynasha stumbled to her feet. With a swift tread, she was at the door, pulling it open. She was prepared to greet the light of candles, the halls beyond, and the sliver of light that so often caught her eye.

Metal fell to the marble floor with a crash.

"Ah!" a voice exclaimed in unison with hers. The silver tray clattered to the stone floor, its contents splayed before her feet, and Vynasha blinked against the silvery glow that blinded her vision.

The light dimmed to reveal nothing but a hunched old man.

His clothing was fashioned in a manner she had not seen before, the tailored coat built as though it had once fit proudly on a soldier's shoulders. His breeches were pulled high and his billowing shirt tucked within, his knee-high boots worn and cracked. His hands trembled as he knelt and cleaned the mess at their feet.

Then she noticed his ears, half hidden by white hair, were pointed sharply. And while his features were almost human, his skin was a deathly gray, his figure so transparent that she could almost make out the hall through him.

For a moment, Vynasha could only stare, for he looked as she had always imagined a ghost would. As he moved, a sliver of white light emanated from his skin and followed him like a halo. She knew that gleam, the same she'd briefly seen within the gatekeeper.

"It's you," she whispered. "You're the one who's been watching over me."

Slowly, he lifted his head to look at her. Vynasha feared he would flee. Her shift pooled over the floor and the upturned tray as she knelt to meet him. Could he be the one she remembered amid whatever fever had taken her memory after her encounter with the beast?

"Are you Odym?"

His mouth opened, and he breathed in deeply before nodding warily. "How do you know that name?"

Vynasha cocked her head as she righted the silver tray and began picking up the mess. "Did he ask you to keep a watch on me?"

Odym glanced down at either end of the darkened hall behind before turning to her. "Best let me take that and fetch a fresh tray, Mistress."

"So I'm right," she murmured. "Not that I'm surprised. Can't have your *guests* running into trouble? Or running away."

Fresh fear made his wrinkles deeper, and he returned the contents of her breakfast to its tray urgently before standing.

"Not so fast," she grumbled as she climbed to her feet.

Odym gasped as Vynasha caught the lapel of his coat and tugged him inside. She shut the wooden door and rested her back against it.

For a breath, they held one another's gaze.

Okay, you got him in here. Now what?

Odym kept his gaze averted and stammered his protests. "This is *most* inappropriate. You have not even dressed…"

Vynasha huffed a sigh as she interrupted his tirade. "Here, let me take that."

His mouth opened when she stole the tray from his hands and set it down on the nearby table.

"You should not do such things," he said. "Master would be most displeased."

She bristled. "I've been cleaning my own messes all my life, thank you. I never asked to be fed and treated like a pet."

He did not answer her, choosing instead to bow his head and barely conceal his discomfort.

She rolled her eyes. "Odym," she began again then paused to find his eyes upon the pages of Soraya's book on the rug behind her. "How long have you served in this castle?"

He pulled his attention from the book with great effort and whispered, "A very long time."

"I'm not the first prisoner your master has taken, am I?" she pressed.

Odym looked to the walls, as though fearful of what they might whisper. "No."

"What happened to the other prisoner who stayed in this room, Soraya? Did she escape?"

"She… faded." His voice shook as he tucked his chin into the lapel of his coat.

"So she didn't escape?"

"No, milady."

Vynasha's hopes sank to the pit of her belly. Would she fade too if she displeased Ferox? Had she crossed mountains through the heart of winter only to die here, become another soul lost to the mysterious Wylder Mountains?

"Do you wish to leave us?" he tentatively asked.

"I only made this journey because I thought I would find my brother." Vynasha hesitated. "And I didn't come to Wylderland alone." She moved to lean against the wooden bedpost to rest her bad leg. "I should have listened to Wolfsbane. If I'd known the price of your master's hospitality…"

"Wolfsbane?" Odym asked, startling her. "You know that wretch?" His brow wrinkled into a frown when he saw her need to pursue the matter further. "I… forgive me, milady. I am sorry, but I have much to do."

"Go? But can't you stay just a little longer? If you know Wolfsbane, maybe you met my brother, Ceddrych?" She moved to cut off his escape route.

Odym shook his head and muttered, "No, no, Mistress, please do not ask questions I may not answer."

Vynasha dug her nails into her palms. "I see."

Ferox ordered them not to tell me, so Ceddrych must have come here. But why the secrecy?

Odym moved easily around her, his boots barely lingering on the carpet.

Before his hand could meet the latch, she called after him, "Wait! When I first came here, I left a pack in one of the halls. Many of the objects inside were irreplaceable. They're all I have left of my life, and I… would be grateful if you could check with the servants to see about finding it."

Odym tilted his head curiously before nodding. "I shall do what I can, Mistress. And I shall endeavor to avoid dropping your tray when next I come," he said as he opened the door and let it fall shut behind him.

CHAPTER THIRTEEN

A Tempting Offer

VYNASHA STIRRED FROM dreamless sleep when her door creaked open some time later. Her hand closed around the knife she'd swiped from her breakfast tray beneath her pillow and winced, hissing as the wounds in her stomach twinged.

Familiar whispers followed the heavy thud of something set before the fireplace. "Poor Odym seemed most troubled, did he not, Myrel?"

Only the maids, Vynasha thought with relief. Her dreams had been troubled, her limbs stiff from aches and pains she earned from her stupidity the night before.

"Wonder if he's worried over Grendel again, though why he pities the fool I shall never know. Easy, Myrel, you'll spill," the maid hissed before the two women practically floated back through the door with a gentle click of the lock.

Who is Grendel?

Vynasha groaned as she pushed aside the covers, shivering in the chill draft sweeping in from the nearby window. Snow fell in heavy sheets beyond the glass, the sunlight a warm amber glow that alighted over the round bath the maids had drawn and left before the fire.

She glanced between the door and the tapestry covering the hidden passage. The girl in the tapestry had her back to Vynasha, once again busy smelling hedges filled with roses. Vynasha undressed as quickly as she could. She hadn't bothered to don the dress from earlier after Odym's visit. She winced as the soft fabric stuck to her bloody skin on its way to joining the pile before the hearth.

More to burn, she thought as she added the small clothes, stockings, and stays to the fire. Her cry echoed through the room as she sank into the steaming water. She couldn't recall the last time she'd had a bath. When Tamyra drew her one above Mayve's Tavern?

Tears squeezed past her closed eyelids as she sank back, careful to keep her hair free of the water. The heady scent of magick and rosewater filled her nose. She gasped as the cuts in her abdomen from the beast's claws burned, the skin tightening. Her hand pressed over the wound, only to find the scabs gone and her flesh slowly mending once more.

Her startled gasp and the slosh of water seemed too loud as she watched every recent cut and scratch heal within the water.

If only we'd had this after the fire, came the bitter thought.

Vynasha closed her eyes and gripped the sides of the tub, pulling her wandering mind back to the present. To the diary and key she'd hidden under her pillow alongside the breakfast knife. To the beastly prince she would be expected to sup with soon, judging from the fine dress clothes and jewels the maids had laid out for her.

If Odym could not give her answers and Ferox was unwilling, she needed to seek the answers herself.

Bide your time and play their game.

The gatekeeper had promised to help her, but people often made oaths to achieve their own goals. Vynasha would make whatever vows she needed if it helped her escape this cursed place.

All the aches and pains she'd felt from the previous night and the journey before were seeped away by the enchanted water. She rose with a strength she hadn't felt in over a year. Vynasha opened her wardrobe and stared at her scarred body, at the way her bad leg appeared straighter, not so twisted. Did the scars, worse at her chest and arms, seem less prominent and rigid?

Vynasha covered her chest with a shiver and turned to the gold dress waiting for her, velvet and silk and a sheer glittering fabric she'd never seen before. A faint burn of magick pinched her nose as she lifted the skirts. A glance at her window and the waning rosy light of day reminded her she needed to hurry.

The bodice clung to her and pushed her breasts to their fullest. The sleeves trailed past her wrists, enough that she might be able to hide her makeshift dagger, and the skirts puffed out in a velvety train. She ran her fingers through her curls as best she could before shutting her wardrobe and pulling on her preferred boots.

The door clicked and opened on its own before her hand met the knob. Chills laced her spine as Vynasha entered the hall just beyond and the door fell shut.

The candles standing vigil outside her door flickered, so the golden halo around her shuddered as she left the safety of her domain. The castle drew its breath as Vynasha followed the marked trail of candles. Her fist stayed wrapped around the handle of the dinner knife, flipped so the blade lay against her inner arm.

A pressure weighed against her shoulders, and chills darted up her neck. And from deep within the shadows, a warm wind blew across her flesh. Vynasha ran a hand over the constrictive bodice, over the newly healed skin of her stomach, and marveled at the strength in her limbs, the absence of her usual limp.

She jumped when the door waiting at the end of the familiar journey opened on its own. She gladly welcomed the gargoyles clutching torches high above and the dragon skulls that grinned down at her. Against the glow of candles, shadows danced. Other floors of the castle jutted out just shy of the massive chandelier, and she could almost see the ghostly faces watching her arrival. She cringed and averted her gaze.

"A good night's rest has done you wonders, Beauty." Ferox's gravelly voice greeted her. He waited just behind her high-backed chair with a smirk on his wolfish features. His green eyes reflected the nearby candles with an animal's sheen, and she thought briefly of the curse. He didn't dress like a beast, certainly. Tonight, he wore threads of autumnal shades.

"Sit and feast, if you please." A long-fingered hand extended toward the food steaming from a place setting at the long table.

Vynasha sat in the proffered chair without protest and frowned as he lifted her easily, chair and all, to tuck her in. He walked with such ease on two legs that it was impossible to compare him to the creature who had haunted her steps through the castle. His silver fur contrasted with her golden dress, and she wondered for a moment how he might look on a frozen mountainside, bedecked in white and howling at the moon.

"Forgive my absence this day. I had fully intended on offering a proper tour of your new home. Yet there has been trouble with our borders, and my apparent neglect has led some to believe me careless." He observed her as though he wanted to peel apart her layers and taste what was underneath.

Vynasha drank from the goblet beside her plate, suddenly thirsty. "You don't need to entertain me, Beast."

Ferox's emerald eyes flashed, a hint of a smile revealing too-sharp teeth. "Trust me when I say I would much prefer your company, Beauty."

Vynasha swallowed another bite of meat far richer than any she'd had before. As difficult as it was to eat a polite portion of each plate, she barely contained the moan behind her bite. Ferox's lips curled higher, ears twitching beside golden horns, as though he *knew*.

"Tell me…" She cleared her throat and lifted her chin. "Do you whisper in the ears of your subjects the way you did mine? Maybe your borders would cause less trouble if you gave your people more freedom."

"Freedom is a luxury few can afford." Ferox dragged the chair at the opposite end of the table free before settling down with effortless grace. "And would it be so hard to believe if I told you that you were the exception, Beauty?"

Vynasha rolled her eyes. "I know I'm not the first guest to your halls." She lifted the strand of sapphires dangling from her throat in clear implication and relished the way his beastly grin turned to a grimace.

"And yet you are the first I am asking to become my wife," he said with a click of his claws.

Vynasha choked on her wine and snatched the edge of the tablecloth to catch the drops from her chin before she could ruin the dress. "Are you mad? I can't be your wife!"

"Why not?" came his heavy reply.

"Because you're a *beast*, and I'm… Well, look at me!"

A monster.

Ferox's sigh rumbled through the room like a wave. "And if I tell you that you *must* marry me, to buy your freedom?"

Blood rushed through her with the accompanying heat that sometimes rose unbidden. Vynasha clenched her jaw and forced it to relax enough to say, "So I have no choice."

The flames danced upon the candelabrum between them as Ferox chuckled. "A choice is precisely what I am trying to give to you, Beauty. You may not believe me when I say you are an exception, but I beg you to think on what I am offering you."

"And what is that?"

"Power." Ferox's deep voice echoed through the hall, burrowing beneath her skin, an echo at the back of thoughts she'd never tempted.

Mother had always preached caution. The villagers might tolerate small magicks, but never should she allow her inner creature loose. She chewed on her lip as she met Ferox's waiting gaze.

"Tell me, what is it that you want, Beauty?"

"I—" She sputtered and forced herself to pick up her glass and down a mouthful of wine, correctly this time. Only after she set the glass down did she lift her gaze. "I don't want to be trapped inside my room all day."

"I will create paths that will be safe for you if you wish. What else?"

"I want to see my horse."

"I shall take you to visit him on the morrow," Ferox intoned then paused with a grin. "Surely that cannot be all. Tell me, what is it you really *want?*"

Vynasha pushed back her chair and stood, bracing her hands on the table. "I want to find my brother."

Ferox inclined his head, golden horns gleaming in the candlelight. "You may have already guessed that I am bound by powers I cannot control, but I *am* the master of this castle, of these lands. If you accept my proposal, I will not only protect you, but I can and shall find your brother. Only give me his name and consider it done."

"If I accept you, you mean," she said as she slowly approached him. The knife hidden up her sleeve gave her comfort, but she did not fear the beastly prince as she should. And if he truly wanted her…

"Why do you want me?"

Ferox's jaws clicked shut, yet the way his gaze swept over her, as though he did not see her scars but who she was beneath, caused her breath to catch in her throat. "Give me your brother's name, and I shall prove my good intentions, Beauty."

"What else would you give me if I said yes?" She drew in an unsteady breath and paused before his chair.

Ferox leaned forward and held out a clawed hand to her. "A home for you and your family if you wish it."

She closed her eyes at the unexpected wave of heartache. How she had longed for that sense of home. She had led Dragos and Wyll into the mountains, seeking Ceddrych in hope of it.

Vynasha opened her eyes and placed her hand over his furred palm. "His name is Ceddrych," she said and startled as his clawed thumb grazed her uneven skin.

She shivered as his gravelly voice rumbled. "I shall find him, and then I shall show you how powerful you were born to be."

Vynasha wasn't expecting Odym to be waiting for her as she left the dining hall and Ferox's company behind. Her eyes widened as the luminous man beckoned her to follow him with a tremulous smile.

"Did you find my things?" she asked.

Odym shook his head. "And we are not like to, Mistress. Too many roam the halls freely, I fear."

"Thank you for looking." Vynasha wrapped her arms around her chest and glanced at the shadows around them. "I'm assuming you're allowed to speak with me now." She easily kept pace alongside the man, eyes drawn to the pointed tips of his ears again.

"Master has given his leave." Odym wrung his hands together and kept watch over their surroundings.

"You told him?"

"Of course! It is far better for Master to hear of my failure from my own words than others."

Vynasha fisted her skirts and glanced up to the balconies with a sigh. "He certainly seems to have won your loyalty."

Odym spared her an uneasy glance. "He keeps us safe from

that which seeks to harm us. We owe him our lives, milady. We would have faded long ago were it not for Master Ferox."

"Please, call me Vynasha." She fingered the hilt of the knife against her wrist and eyed the shadows.

"As you wish, Mistress Vynasha."

Her sudden laugh seemed to push the shadows back and shocked her as much as it clearly did Odym. Vynasha covered her mouth and shook her head. "Saints above, I'm going to go mad in this place. All of you must be mad. Between the walls whispering and your master's marriage proposal…"

"He has asked you already?" Odym interrupted, surprise etched into his craggy face.

"In truth, it wasn't the worst proposal I've ever heard," she muttered. Not that anyone had ever asked for Vynasha's hand, not even before the fire took what beauty she might have claimed. Her magick had always made her too strange for the local folk. But her sisters had drawn plenty of attention and countless proposals of every nature.

They turned down the hall leading to her bedchambers, and Vynasha slowed her steps as she added, "Even if he is under some curse, I don't know if I can learn to love a beast."

Odym cleared his throat and swayed slightly. "Master Ferox is kind to offer… much as our former mistress had a choice."

"You mean Soraya?" The air thickened, and the door to her bedroom gently creaked open.

Odym's form shivered and, for a moment, thinned before Vynasha caught his arm. He was less solid than he should have been, but she still managed to get a grip on his coat sleeve.

He looked at her, incredulous. "Mistress, please, I misspoke. I should return to my duties…"

Vynasha ignored his protests as she dragged the old man into her room and shut the door with a firm shove. She glanced at the freshly lit fire and clear evidence the maids had done their work while she was away. Magick, both dark and light, seemed to press upon them, and Vynasha narrowed her gaze at the way the tapestry rippled. Odym's arm trembled beneath her hold, and he looked up at her with a wary gaze.

"I'm not a fool," she whispered. "I know you're all bound under some dark enchantment. But if I accept your master's proposal, I will be your new mistress, won't I? Now, tell me about Soraya."

Odym flinched as though her words truly held the power Ferox promised. "Mistress was a Fayere princess in her land. She agreed to marry the king because she believed he loved her."

"And did he?" she threw back.

"No," Odym firmly said. "What he loved was her power and that she would give him control over the window between our land and hers. He wanted to possess and control her."

Vynasha removed her hand from Odym's arm. "And does your master love power as well?"

Again, the strange blend of respect and fear filled Odym's expression. "Master Ferox is not as the king was and certainly not as terrible as you imagine. He has done much to keep the peace between our peoples."

"Maybe you're right, but I'll have to wait and see for myself." Vynasha's leg throbbed as she crossed the room and sank onto the rug before the fireplace. "If you've nothing else to say besides your master's praises, you may leave."

The heat suffused her limbs as the smoke filled the air with the scent of fir and cinnamon. She didn't bother turning to watch Odym leave and so startled as the older man sank slowly onto the rug beside her with a creaking sigh.

A faint smile tilted the corner of his face, an echo of fine and noble features in the expression. "It is unwise to speak much of *her*. But if you will not hear accolades of Master Ferox, would you like to hear a tale of the land as it was before?"

"Am I not keeping you from your other duties?" she asked, the ghost of a grin tugging at her cheek.

Odym smiled. "Master does not require my services this evening. This time is my own."

She nodded, and rather than ask him the questions she really wanted, she listened.

"Once, a long time ago, the window between our land and another was open. Like a mirror, this world looked remarkably akin to ours, and some of its people might have come from here originally. Or mayhap it was us who came from them in the beginning. That knowledge, like the name of this mirror world, has been lost." He reached into the fire to shift the logs. Vynasha's eyes widened as his hand emerged from the flames unscathed.

"Folk from both our side and theirs came and went as they pleased," he continued, "but none were allowed to stay. It would never do to have the wylderfolk living here when the mirror land was so different from ours. For in this other land, men were greedy and punished because of it. As they diminished, the other peoples changed. And beasts that could already walk and talk became stronger and wiser. The wielders of true magick were able to take control of the kingdoms again.

"But our people began to go missing before the first war began. We were not as strong as we had been led to believe, and many magick-wielders from the mirror land had made their home in our forest. The leaves turned darker, and the paths grew treacherous, and our people did not go into certain glens for fear of the shadows lurking within. More forgotten kind came through the mirror that we were not aware of, yet our people visited this other land less and less. Soon, there was not a babe born in these mountains who did not possess the blood inside them."

Vynasha listened to his stories deep into the night, until the sound of his voice was replaced by dreams of her mother and words spoken long ago. Only on the verge of sleep once more were they recalled.

"The roses have sensed a change in the wind and will not bloom as before," Wynyth had whispered while her fingers graced Vynasha's brow. *"Mayhap they sense what I cannot foresee. Mayhap an even greater magick is coming."* Her smile grew as she met her daughter's gaze. *"Or mayhap it is already here."*

Chapter Fourteen

A Beast's Nature

I had almost forgotten my mission in coming to this side of the mirror all those years ago. My heart belonged to my wicked husband with his unquenchable passion for my flesh. After the birth of our son, I felt a surge of hope. I could almost pretend that I was not sent here to sabotage this realm and shatter the mirror between our worlds forever.

Soon after our son's birth, the first attacks were reported from the outer villages. Beofric was so furious when he learned it had been caused by people of the blood. He blamed me and said I was a wicked creature. He did not understand that I had come to love this land and its people. For men had been allowed to prosper here and were not as cruel and unfeeling as my kind.

Beofric began the first witch hunts, as he called them, to root out and rid the world of evil magick. I learned to accept his loss of love for me but not from my little one. He stole my son away and vowed to raise him to hate me. How could our son despise his own kind?

YNASHA SHUT THE book with tremulous hands and wondered if Ferox might be the very child Soraya spoke of. Was he truly a beast, as he had suggested? Or was he, too, a victim of the curse and longing to break free, to return to his true form?

She had slept through the maids' appearance that morning and didn't recall falling asleep before the hearth. She felt oddly refreshed, far more used to sleeping on hard surfaces than her cushy bed. Perhaps that was the trick?

A soft knock rapped against the door, and Vynasha was quick to tuck Soraya's diary out of sight. "Coming, Odym," she called as she crossed the room in her stockings and swung open the door, only to freeze at the beast waiting for her on the other side.

"Good morning, Beauty," he said.

"Ferox!" She gripped her skirts, grateful she'd at least donned the red silk dress left out by her maids that morning.

"Pardon the intrusion, but I wondered if you were ready to visit our stable? Your horse has been most anxious in your absence." He towered over her, his horned head above the doorframe. Humor danced in his forest-green eyes as he held out a clawed hand to her.

"Yes! Just… let me fetch my boots." Vynasha ducked her head to hide her smile as she retreated. "I thought you might simply send one of the servants to escort me instead."

"You will soon learn I always keep my promises," Ferox rumbled from the doorway. Much to her relief, he didn't barge in as she half expected.

She ignored the old twinge in her leg as she slipped her boots on and stood. "We'll see," she said as she approached with caution.

The door slipped shut behind them as Ferox stepped aside and held out his arm. "Let us begin small, then." His silver-trimmed coat was soft and thick blue wool.

Vynasha hesitated then placed her scarred hand over his arm. She barely flicked her gaze to his, luminous in the candlelit shadows.

Faint sunlight pierced through windows above the open hall. The castle seemed less oppressive with Ferox's overwhelming presence. Even the walls were silent as they passed carvings and tapestries.

"You have never said my name before," he spoke, startling her from her thoughts and drawing her gaze back to his. "Although I am fond of Beast, I find I prefer Ferox." His smile was not so frightening despite its sharp edges.

Vynasha frowned as they took another turn down a hall she'd never been down before, filled with obsidian statues of mythical creatures. "Maybe if you'd stop calling me Beauty, I wouldn't need to call you Beast."

"As you wish, Beauty." Ferox's chuckle rumbled through his great form and filled the hall with surprising warmth.

Vynasha ducked her head, again hiding behind her curls with a shake of her head. Odym had claimed Ferox wasn't as bad as she believed. Maybe he was right.

They entered through another door, this time into a wide circular tower, and slowly descended the spiraling stair together. Vynasha was grateful for his arm and the railing, untrusting of her bad leg despite whatever tonic they'd slipped into her bath. A year of accidents and injuries had taught her caution.

Her grip tightened on Ferox's arm as she recalled his voice the night of the fire and the other times she'd been near danger after. The day she nearly sliced her toe off after a botched attempt to cut firewood this past winter. The spring she accidentally happened upon bear cubs, and the voice, *his* voice, told her where to run and hide.

Ferox had been in her head for so long, he'd never felt like a stranger. And as they reached the bottom of the tower and Ferox opened the door to reveal the torchlit cave that served as stables, she wondered why he felt like a friend.

When he should be my enemy.

A familiar whinny broke the troubling thought.

"Dragos!" Vynasha released Ferox's arm and rushed as quickly as she could across the warm stable to her old friend's stall.

Dragos tossed his head and whinnied again at her approach, pressing against the wooden gate of his stall. Vynasha threw her arms around his neck and masked her tears in his mane. "I'm sorry! I'm so sorry I couldn't come to see you before. I've missed you so much."

She sensed Ferox approach them before halting to offer them space. She pulled back and took in the fresh hay and grains, the way his coat gleamed in the torchlight in ways she'd never managed to make before. "He looks well," she offered.

Ferox took another step, and oddly enough, Dragos did not seem afraid. "We have done our best to tend to him and give him exercise when the snows allowed."

She dug her hand into Dragos's shaggy winter coat and glanced back at Ferox. "Could I ride him about the grounds?"

Ferox tilted his head, his warm gaze flashing and suddenly masked. "That would not be wise, Beauty. The old fields are no longer safe."

Vynasha turned her back to Ferox, and the old anger returned, flushing through her limbs and banking the fire. "You're afraid I'll run away, you mean?"

Dragos turned his head toward the beastly prince as he approached and rested a hand on the gate of the empty stall beside them. "Forgive me if I am unwilling to gamble with your life," Ferox grumbled.

Her heart ached as she looked Dragos in the eye, as she felt the old horse's need for open skies. "What if you came with me?"

"Would your friend accept my company?" Ferox shifted closer and lifted a clawed hand to hover over Dragos.

Vynasha couldn't say what compelled her to take Ferox's wrist and bring his much larger hand to press against the horse's shuddering chest. Though Dragos's nostrils flared and his hooves picked up slightly, he gave no other sign of discomfort.

Vynasha slowly removed her hand and found Ferox looking at her incredulously. "Is this your magick?" he asked with a shallow breath.

Something warm stirred in her chest, embers of a different fire stirring at the careful way Ferox ran his hand over Dragos's neck. The beastly prince was a portrait of contradictions, inherently deadly yet gentle, underlying ruthlessness. Yet to her, he offered a kindness she did not deserve. What made her so different from the others who had come before?

"I suppose it would be all right if I accompanied you, so long as we stay near to the outer walls and do not approach the forest or the falls," Ferox said. "Do you need a coat? A saddle?"

Vynasha smiled again and shook her head. "I don't really feel the cold anymore, and this blanket will suit us fine."

Ferox seemed reluctant to remove his hand but was quick to open the pen and allow her to bring Dragos out with softly spoken commands.

"Easy, boy, I've got you," she crooned as she beckoned Dragos out of his stall.

"How do you not feel the cold?" Ferox asked as he guided them to an arched door built into the cave side. The great door creaked, and a gust of icy air and sunlight met them beyond the cavern gate.

"I haven't felt much since the fire," she confessed as they ventured into the field.

"*To give life requires sacrifice, little starling,*" Mother had said.

Vynasha sucked in a harsh breath, her scarred lungs struggling as she drew in the scents of the mountains and the winds biting her unscarred cheek. The drift lay so thick every step was a struggle she savored. It felt like ages since she had worked her muscles in such a way. She never would have thought she'd miss it.

Ferox had fallen silent at her words. His voice had been with her that night, and so Vynasha felt an odd kinship with the beastly prince. The question seized in her throat, and she took comfort in Dragos's thick winter coat. She threaded her fingers in his mane to untangle any snares gently and found the courage to speak.

"Your voice woke me." She watched Ferox carefully from the corner of her eye, the way he stiffened and tilted his head to take in their surroundings. "You were watching me that night, somehow. How much have you seen? How much did you already know about me before I made this journey?"

His silence was heavy with words he picked through and discarded until he finally said, "I know that your mother passed her magick on to you, and this led the villagers to call you a witch. And I know you are one of the blood through her. This is what allowed me to see you, as you say, through the mirror."

Heat pressed against her skin with his words as though calling forth the gifts her mother passed to her. "What do you mean, one of the blood?"

Ferox slowed his loping stride, and Dragos came to a stop, nuzzling at the snow to reveal buried grasses. "Many came through the mirror long ago, and when the kingdom fell, there were few who escaped beyond the borders of Wylderland."

"And you believe my mother was descended from them?"

Ferox's teeth gleamed with his smile, the sunlight illuminating his coat and gilded horns against newly fallen snow. His voice lowered to a dim rumble, though they were far beyond the reach of the castle now. "I believe your mother was one who escaped."

"But…" She shook her head and allowed Dragos to lead them along some unseen path, edging closer to the looming forest and away from the nearby cliffs. "I thought the kingdom fell long ago, certainly beyond the memory of my grandmother's generation in Whistleande."

There had been rumors of the dangerous road north, of course. Folk avoided the fading road, though occasionally, there were those foolish enough to brave it. Yet Wynyth had whispered old tales to her, half-remembered fairy tales of monsters and folk of the air. She lifted her gaze to find Ferox watching her with a curiously eager expression, as though he were waiting for something.

"How long has it been since the kingdom fell?" she dared to ask.

Ferox's eyes flashed as though pleased she had asked the right question. "Two hundred and seventy years, Beauty."

Vynasha's teeth chattered with a sudden chill for the first time since leaving the castle. "I think I'm ready to head back."

"Of course, Beauty," Ferox replied and offered his arm to her. She didn't hesitate to take it, to savor the warmth emanating from him. Even as something like shock and fear sliced its way up her spine.

Were the villagers right about us?

If Ferox spoke true, and Wynyth had been one of the *beings* who escaped over two centuries before, did that make Vynasha a monster too?

CHAPTER FIFTEEN

A Garden of Glass and Roses

OVER THE FOLLOWING week, Vynasha fell into an almost leisurely routine. After a lifetime of labor and struggle, she was unaccustomed to steady meals and high walls to shelter behind.

She attempted to fall asleep in the high-canopied bed, only to end up before the hearth most nights. At times, she was awakened from a deep sleep by an urge to walk to her door and listen. Sometimes, she heard nothing, only fought the impulse to open the latch barring the hall. Yet most times, claws dragged on the other side of her door. And she remembered the feeling of soft fur against her cheek, of falling asleep and feeling oddly at peace. Every morning, she woke curled up against the bedroom door. When she tried to think back to the moment her dreams had led her from bed, she only found muddled impressions.

Mornings she spent reading Soraya's diary or badgering Odym into telling her more of the legends of Wylderland. And she did her best not to think too hard about who or what her mother had truly been.

"The people who first settled these mountains were good and pure," he told her. "They came from the Eirwen Mountains to the west, hoping to build new lives away from the tyranny of an evil queen. Together, they built this castle, and it was so filled, it was called a city by some. Everyone was treated fairly, and a golden age began."

Other times, she questioned him about the inner workings of the castle.

"Who prepares the food?"

Odym's shoulders pulled back, and he lifted his bent neck. "There are others like me who still serve Master's bidding."

"And how do you continue to eat when you are so isolated from the rest of the land?"

He smiled cryptically as he answered, "The land serves us well. Coney and grouse abound on the grounds. Plants have always grown here, though our season has not changed since before it happened. And the waters that flow underground were never cursed. So we do well."

As she held his gaze, she thought of Soraya, the other prisoner, and the wondrous strange things she had written. Vynasha had no intention of becoming trapped or fading. No time could be wasted if she were going to make it out of these mountains in the heart of winter.

"Odym," she began, "you told me there are others. I would like to meet them. I would like to see more of the castle from your eyes."

At which the old servant blanched and said, "Surely there is much more you should rather see with Master Ferox."

As for her beastly prince, Vynasha grew accustomed to finding him at her door at odd hours. Each time, he led her along different routes through the endless maze of the castle. They took Dragos outside thrice more before the snows thickened and a blizzard kept beasts and beings locked behind the high walls of the lost city.

After this, Ferox brought her to the glass gardens.

"Have you enjoyed the books I lent you, Beauty?" he asked as he led her through a glass-enclosed tunnel that carried the pathway outside the castle.

"The language is a bit difficult," she confessed. "My brother only taught me a little before he…"

"I would be happy to further your education," Ferox said. "If you please."

"We'll see." Vynasha swallowed the lump in her throat but couldn't tear her gaze away from the glass gardens rising just ahead. It was impossible to contain her marvel over the perfectly fused glass panes and metal frame. Beyond the thin barrier, the snows raged angrily, building high along either side. "How do you keep the cold out?"

"Magick. How else?" he asked with a low rumble that served for a semblance of laughter and pushed the gate leading to the main gardens aside.

Vynasha gasped and drew in dewy, pungent air redolent of roses and other flora. "It's like spring in here." Though truly, she wasn't sure if summers had ever been this warm in Whistleande.

His chuckle made her shiver from her fingertips clasped to his arm and into her bones. "Our former queen crafted this place as a refuge from the castle she saw as a prison."

"It's beautiful." She glanced at his large, claw-toed feet as they stepped out into the root and petal-strewn marble floor. Ferox was like her, discordant between beauty and ugliness, fragility and danger.

Clusters of berries hung from the hedge lining the glass walls, gleaming like drops of blood. Dead shrubs stood in symmetrical rows around a frozen fountain at the center. Snow fell over their heads in waves, sliding off the glass in a heated shimmer. The castle loomed behind them. The tops of the uttermost towers were masked by clouds, yet beyond the glass walls, she glimpsed white fields dotted with fir trees and rimmed by the ancient wood. The forest line was so clear she could almost feel it calling to her. What would Ferox do if she left him now and simply ran? What if she kept running until the drifts swallowed her up and prayed Wolfsbane found her again?

"Have you had any luck searching for Ceddrych?" She removed her fingers from his arm and clasped her hands behind her back as they walked toward the lifeless fountain.

"I fear we will need more time, but our territory is far vaster than you may realize. Your brother could also be hiding among the mountain folk who choose to hunt us rather than live among us," he added with a slight snarl.

Vynasha shook her head. Wolfsbane would have told her if Ceddrych had been hiding with them, wouldn't he?

Ferox took her uneasy silence for a different kind of fear. "I know it is not the news you hoped to hear, but these things take time, Beauty."

"I know," she said, a faint rasp dragging the sound through her throat.

They circled the fountain slowly together. "Would you tell me more about your family, the valley you hail from beyond our borders?"

She rolled her shoulders. "Couldn't you just see it all in my mind?"

Ferox chuffed with a beast's approximation of a laugh. "I was not always watching, Beauty. And I am not a mind reader in case you had any doubts."

Vynasha lifted her chin and wondered if she could ever fully trust him, though he felt more like her friend than her captor. Ferox met her gaze, and again, it was his kindness that led her to answer.

"My father had been married, when he was still Lord of North Hill, to a local noblewoman. They had four children together and were expecting a fifth when the king put his sword to my grandfather's neck and cursed his line forever. My father lost his wife and the babe first. The village folk said it was the curse. Father was so brokenhearted, he left his remaining children in his mother's care and took to traveling to oversee what little remained of the family trade. That's how he met my mother on the road to the Eastern Eirwens. Folk later said she must have bewitched him."

"And did she?" Ferox asked with a sharp-toothed grin.

Vynasha shook her head. "It didn't help that while he was away, the forest swallowed up the manor, along with every soul who lived there. Folk said it was the curse, too, but I think my grandmother was tired of living so far from Whistleande and preferred the village."

Vynasha stared at the fine boots on her feet and their overlapping, fur-lined cloaks and remembered she was the guest of a prince now. "Grandmother Mayve eventually turned the first floor of her village home into a tavern using what was left of our coffers. My father and mother helped until Mayve gave them money to buy tools and a wagon. They built our first home closer to the forest than anyone else dared dwell, but the villagers called us cursed, even after my parents were gone."

"I am sorry for the hardship you have suffered, Beauty. I, too, understand this burden. I, too, carry my people's legacy." Ferox lifted his wolf-like nose to the towers and parapets behind them, and something about his words sent chills down her spine. "Yet we shall have the final victory when we are wed. I have waited so long for the end to this madness, and I would wait still another age if it meant I could see this turn to *ruin*."

Vynasha followed his gaze to the castle looming behind them like a dark specter. "What happened to your family, Beast?"

"Butchered like cattle," he growled. "Others fled like cowards, and still, there are some that haunt the forests."

Echoes of howls in the wind compelled her gaze to return to the black forest.

Vynasha could not later say what bade her reach for him. Her hand was upon his clawed hand, fingers wrapping around his and bringing his startled gaze back to her. "You've been alone," she stated.

Like Wyll and I were alone.

Ferox's warm hand curled around hers. "But we do not need to be alone anymore."

She swallowed back the urge to tell him about Wyll, to explain all the thoughts she hadn't somehow sent to him across such vast distances. How had he done it? How was such a thing possible?

Ferox chuckled as though he had seen the questions in her face. "Come. There is something else I wish to show you."

He led her down a different corner path that was lined with rows of rosebushes. Though they were much larger than any she or Wynyth had grown in their valley, Vynasha was compelled to step closer and brush her fingertips against the black stems.

"You know this flower, I believe," Ferox teased.

Vynasha slipped her hand from his and knelt to the rich earth beside the path. She brushed aside fallen leaves and dirt to reach the roots. The magick in her blood stirred at the touch, the ache in her limbs a dull throb because she hadn't turned the energy to use in too long. And the roses called back to her through the earth, a song of pain and endless sorrow. "This bush needs tending." Vynasha blinked back tears as she whispered, "They all do."

Ferox swept his clawed hands out grandly. "Then I shall place you in charge, Beauty. The roses of this garden belong to you and you alone from this moment forward. And if you wish, I can allow the path you came by here to remain open, so you may come and tend them every morning at your leisure."

She turned with a start. "That is… this is too much."

"Nothing is too much for you, Beauty." He crouched to meet her and scooped one of her hands into his. "I promised you your heart's desire, and you shall have it and more."

Perhaps it wouldn't be so bad to marry this beast after all.

"I should like to spend my mornings here," she hedged. "And

I think I would like a moment alone if it is agreeable to you." As he studied her, she forced her breathing to remain even and her face to appear open.

At last, he smiled and squeezed her hand lightly. "I shall see you at dinner then, Beauty." His shadow fell over her as he rose to watch her scatter more snow from the buds. "Here, you may use this until I have arranged for you to have the proper tools."

She turned and gasped when he proffered an ornate dagger. The blade was marked with engravings in an archaic tongue. The hilt was almost black and studded with jewels. Vynasha breathed deeply as she plucked the blade from his hand and wrapped her fingers around the hilt. Only a fool would give their prisoner a weapon… unless he truly saw her as his ally.

"I shall be close at hand. Should you have need of me, you only need to call my name." Ferox's voice rumbled with the sudden thunder in the snow clouds overhead.

"I will," Vynasha absently replied as the beastly prince turned and left the gardens with a soft, loping tread.

Her fingers clenched the hilt until the gems imprinted her skin. "I've lost nearly everything I ever loved," she whispered to the dagger and the roses, to the wylderwood watching her from afar.

Her gaze returned to the dying rosebush with its black thorns, and magick burned hotly in her veins as she ran her hands over the prickled stems. "I won't let you die too," she said as she began to nick the edges off the dead stems.

"I won't let us rot any longer. We're going to live," she breathed as she crawled to the next bush and continued her work. "There's only one way out of this now, Mother: to fight until we are free again. I will find Wyll and see him made whole again."

Her fingers were bloody by the time she finished her row, and sweat trickled down her back from the unnatural heat within the glass gardens. Distantly, the wolves howled, and when she lifted her gaze, pairs of glowing eyes watched her from the forest edge. As she wiped her hands on her skirts, the stems began budding until they bloomed crimson petals the same shade as her blood.

The cuts on her hands still bled hours after she returned to her room from a brief supper with the prince.

She had tugged a pair of discarded gloves up her arms before rushing to meet Ferox and slipped her new dagger around the garter against her thigh. She had almost forgotten about the blade and her hands until she returned to her room and hissed to peel off the sticky fabric. Rather than trying to save them, she threw the ruined gloves into the flames.

"I should learn where they do their washing unless I plan on burning the entire wardrobe," she murmured to the girl in the tapestry. Tonight, the maiden was glancing coyly over her shoulder with a knowing smile.

The tapestry rippled, and the whisper hiss of stone shifting followed as the door behind opened. Vynasha hiked up her skirts and pulled her dagger free. She stumbled back on her sore leg as silvery light peeked through the seams of fabric, then out of the shadows stepped the gatekeeper.

He scowled at the tapestry, muttering under his breath in the old tongue.

"What are you doing here?" She clenched her fists and remembered the dagger too late.

He paused, gaze sweeping over her before settling at the hands she hid behind her back. "Do you know how to use that?" His luminous form rippled and shook as though he were trying to keep himself rooted to the floor.

Vynasha stared back at him as fresh blood seeped from the cuts in her palm and fingers, coating the dagger's hilt. "What are you talking about?" She jumped when his trembling increased and he flew across the room, stopping just shy of her hands. She scowled. "What are you doing?"

"Little fool, I can smell you," he hissed as he took hold of her by the wrists and dragged her hands between them. His nostrils flared as he eyed the bloody dagger. And the fact she had yet to relinquish her grip. "Who gave you this?"

"Excuse me?"

"Who cut you?" he demanded. Vynasha struggled to pull her hands away, but he only held on tighter.

"No one!" She flinched when his head lifted and silver eyes bored into hers.

"How could you be so careless as to spill your own blood in this place?" he muttered and tugged her across the room to the porcelain washbasin by her bed.

"The thorns were sharp," she replied, earning another glare from him.

His forehead creased as he dipped the cloth and washed her free hand. The water in the basin swirled with crimson until it looked the same shade as the roses she had left behind. As he finished cleaning her left hand, he lifted a narrowed gaze to the dagger clenched in her right.

"Fine," she sighed as she placed the dagger on the marble stand beneath the basin.

The gatekeeper's jaw worked as he proceeded to clean her right hand. "Who gave you that blade?"

"Not that it's any of your business, but at least Ferox gave me something to protect myself with," she murmured.

"Mayhap you should have used the blade on *him*," he practically growled as he set the rag aside and something cool and rough pressed into her palms.

"Maybe I should use it on *you*," she countered, then gasped as light emanated from between them, and his larger hands glowed as they caressed hers. With every swipe of his open palm, she felt another stab of pain and watched as he, too, winced.

"W-what are you doing?" she asked and then shivered as another wave of needle pricks bit into her flesh. His eyes squeezed shut briefly. All too suddenly, he released her. Only then did his eyes meet hers as the light that had emanated from his palms seeped into his gray eyes until they too faded into the same incandescence as before. He stared at her curiously as she inspected her hands and found them as clean as before the roses pricked them. Only the old burn scars remained.

Magick requires sacrifice. A voice like her mother's filled her mind, an echo of a memory.

"Gone," she whispered and lowered her hands. "What magick is this?"

"Why should I share my secrets with a witch brainless enough to not wear gloves while working in her garden?"

"Why should I trust your word when I don't even know your name? Now, tell me how you healed my cuts," she replied as she picked up the dagger and held it in a loose grasp at her side.

"My name is Grendel," he finally said. "And you are incapable of wielding magick such as mine."

"According to who?" She took careful steps back before resuming her seat before the hearth. The dagger she held in her lap, unwilling to release the gift he so obviously detested.

"No one this side of the Veil can heal as I can," he simply said. To her surprise, Grendel sank onto the fur rug, close enough for her to maim should she wish it.

"Why?" She was curious now and observed him with careful eyes. His pants were stitched in strange patterns and the boots fashioned from thick black leather. The coat he wore was tattered, though once, it might have been very fine indeed, of a fashion an age past.

He seemed better suited to the role of a courtier than that of a gaoler. She pressed on at his obvious reluctance. "Why are you different?"

He hung his head until his dark hair shadowed his gray brow. "Must you argue and question at every turn?"

"I don't know you," she retorted. "And you don't know me. Forgive me for not trusting you blindly, *Grendel*."

"Yet you blindly trust the word of Ferox?"

"He's given me far more reason to trust than you," she argued. "Ferox has promised to help me."

"Help you?" Grendel scoffed, pushing one long leg out and propping his elbow on his knee. "That monster would ask you to sacrifice your humanity."

Her mood darkened. "He's not a monster. And don't pretend you're worried about my *humanity*. My own people barely considered me human." Vynasha stared at her palm and hoped he would not see her tears.

"What gave you those scars?"

She looked up at him, startled. "I… a fire." He frowned, and the urge to tell him was suddenly on the tip of her tongue. She owed him nothing except he had healed her and asked for nothing in return.

Vynasha studied the rubies in the hilt of her dagger as the words spilled haltingly from her. "I smelled the smoke from the woods and ran back when I saw the light, like the sky was on fire. The flames were so big I shouldn't have gone in, but all I could think about was my sister and nephew. I could hear Wyll screaming, smell them burning. I barely had time to grab him and escape before the house collapsed…" She closed her eyes and remembered the wood that had burned her back and pierced her skin. Her breathing grew labored as she remembered the thick taste of smoke on her tongue.

"Where is your nephew now?"

She turned to the sliver of moonlight shining through the window. "Out there, somewhere. I had to leave him behind before coming here. He's… safe, for now. And I'm only staying here until Ferox finds my brother. Then we can make a new home…"

"You really are a complete imbecile, aren't you?" Grendel snapped. "What exactly did you promise him in return?"

Vynasha's grip tightened on her dagger. "When he finds Ceddrych and brings him here, I'll marry him."

Grendel's features visibly darkened, and the room seemed to dip in temperature, and the fire sputtered in the hearth. "And who has he sent to search for Ceddrych? No one."

She stood and took a step closer to the flames. "How would you know? You're just the gaoler."

Grendel rose smoothly and stalked forward. "I am the gatekeeper of this castle, and I swear to you none have left the castle since your arrival, not even Ferox. He *lied* to you, Vynasha. He has been lying ever since you arrived."

"No!" Vynasha pressed her dagger against his neck. "You're lying."

Grendel's throat constricted against the blade. "Believe what you want, then. Allow that creature to bide his time and draw you under his thrall, and you will *turn*, just like all the others!"

"I am no one's thrall," she snapped then gasped as a bead of blood the shade of violets met the dagger's edge. She stumbled back and stared at the cut she had made. The first time she had willingly harmed another person. The same man who had, moments ago, healed her and now pressed a hand to his neck, watching her with an inscrutable expression.

"Even if you're right," she whispered, "how would I escape when the walls seem to be watching me?"

Grendel closed the distance between them again, to her surprise. "I do not wish to see you meet the same fate as the others, Vynasha. And I would see you free of this cursed place now if I could."

All fight and fury fled at his confounding words, at the possibility that he was speaking the truth. "Why? Why are you really doing this?"

"It does not matter, not anymore." His hand came away coated in a faintly luminous sheen of violet blood. "My blood, your blood, *our* blood. You have bound us together by that blade, and if there is any power left in me, it will grant you access to every door in this castle, to every gate in this city. If you are wise, you will leave posthaste."

Vynasha stared at his outstretched hand and understood for the first time what he could offer her. "I'm not leaving tonight. Ferox made a promise, and until he breaks it, I'll stay. If you're wrong and he finds my brother, it will have all been worthwhile, you see?"

Grendel's fist closed and dropped to his side. "I see you are more of a fool than I believed. But you are so very young, Vynasha. You will learn the truth soon enough, and I will be waiting when you are ready for answers."

She turned to the fireplace with a huff and gripped the blade that held their blood. The truth of his words hummed in the steel humming against her palm, flush with her magick and the foreign pulse of his. "How do I know you aren't the liar, Grendel?"

But when she turned to face him again, the gatekeeper was already gone.

CHAPTER SIXTEEN

A Song of Peace

SHE WOKE TO the sound of firewood crackling and hushed voices whispering.

"Poor dear must have had an awful night, Lyttia," the soft-spoken maid said.

Lyttia was not so keen on keeping her voice down.

"Mud and blood stuck all over her skirts. Would you look at this? Tracked it in as well, no doubt. At least the carpet already gobbled up the evidence. I do not think Master had this in mind when he gave her leave to visit the gardens."

"Is she dead? She looks so pale… ouch! You needn't strike me."

"Serves you right, wishing our mistress ill, Myrel," Lyttia barked.

"But, Lyttia…"

"Hush now! She's waking up soon, and we have little time to right this."

Vynasha kept silent while they changed her out of her skirts.

Their touch was so light, her limbs felt as though they were being guided on air. She could scarcely remember the last time she had been cared for so tenderly. Images of Wynyth's warm hands passed her mind's eye.

"Careful with her head," Lyttia admonished as Vynasha was settled back onto a freshly puffed pillow. "Master will not like that she used blood on the roses…" Lyttia muttered as they drifted away.

"What about the prophecy?" Myrel said.

"You shall wish you had never been birthed if you speak one more word, Myrel Blacktree!"

"Yes, Lyttia," a cowed Myrel simpered.

Vynasha waited until she heard the click of the door announcing their departure before she opened her eyes to the sun shining over her bed. It was rare for the golden rays to gleam so strongly through the dusky windowpanes. Day and night blurred together this far at the top of the world.

As she rose from the bed and into the sunlight, a pleasant warmth stemmed from where Grendel had healed her cuts. The memory made her skin flush with heat and a desperate need to feel sharp winds and stinging thorns on her fingertips.

Vynasha donned fresh undergarments and stockings and ignored the fine dress Lyttia and Myrel had laid out for the day. She ransacked the wardrobe for a pair of gloves and tied her hair back at the nape with a ribbon before slipping the Prince's dagger into the makeshift strap on her leg.

The fire still burned hotly in the fireplace, though she had yet to learn how they kept so many logs and candles burning constantly. Something shifted at the corner of her vision, and she turned to glare as the tapestry rippled and changed.

The maiden in the fabric had her back to her still, but now, she was walking among the roses, and her chin was turned ever so slightly, that she might peek through her long hair. Vynasha stared in shock as the fabric rippled with enchantment as the girl pulled a silver dagger from before her dress and raised her other hand. With one swift movement, she sliced open her palm, and scarlet coated the roses in the tapestry before her until the pale earth was awash with it.

Vynasha turned away from the tapestry with a grimace. "It's just a bloody enchantment. It doesn't mean anything," she muttered as she slipped a candle from its perch beside her door and fled the safety of her room.

Keening wails disrupted the quiet of the house. Though the whispering walls were silent, her attention lingered on the other tapestries covering the stone hall. Stitching rippled as clothes shifted and their hands moved, pointing to her the way she should go.

It was a relief when she at last passed through the hedge into the glass garden. Vynasha let the scent of growth and molt wash over her, the constant cycle of life. Mountains rose beyond the glass, as insurmountable as they appeared yesterday.

Even if I escaped the boundaries of the castle, how long until Wolfsbane found my scent?

She slowed when flashes of colored lights disrupted the dawning sun.

"It is beautiful, is it not?"

Vynasha reached instinctively for her dagger and whirled around until her gaze settled on a pale figure just ahead.

The girl lifted her hand beseechingly but slowly, as if she were fighting against an invisible force. "Forgive me, mistress. I did not mean to startle you."

"Who are you?" Vynasha took a tentative step closer to the girl and made out her ragged clothes, hair black in the dawning light over a pale face. Her limbs were so thin that she appeared little more than a child, with dark eyes too large for her delicate face.

"Hvalla. I tend the garden, keep it clean. But I have not the gift to make things grow." Hvalla closed the distance between them, her form nearly transparent. "But Master brought you here, and I watched you bring them back to life. I have never seen one of the wylderfolk do this. Only one other had the gift, and she hailed from beyond the Veil." Hvalla gasped and folded her hands together tightly in front of her bodice. "My apologies, mistress. I have spoken too freely."

"No, wait, it's all right. I don't mind," Vynasha said as she followed Hvalla to the bushes she'd bled over tending. Unbidden, she thought of the lady in the tapestry, bleeding over the roses in a similar garden.

"See what your magick has done," Hvalla whispered with a crooked smile.

Vynasha frowned and sank to her knees before the budding blooms. The rosebushes, which had been bare and lifeless just yesterday, were now fully bloomed and giving off a ruby gleam. "How is this possible? My roses back home never grew this quickly."

Or bloody glowed.

She didn't notice Hvalla had taken a seat beside her until the girl interrupted her thoughts. "Our magick is strongest here, so close to the Veil. Now that you are home, you can bring the garden back to life. I have waited so long for you, mistress. We all have. I have kept these gardens so when you came, they would be ready to heal and grow. The others are not convinced you are the one foretold by the enchantress. But I *knew* as soon as you brought her roses back to life."

Vynasha stared at the strange girl with the pointed ears and dull gray skin and marveled aloud, "Foretold?"

Hvalla gave her a sad smile and reached out to cover her gloved hand with her palm. Vynasha could see the fabric of her glove through Hvalla's hand.

"Yes, mistress. The enchantress was sorry for the pain she

brought to us in the end. So she made a promise that one day, one who possessed the blood would revoke the curse and mend the mirror."

Vynasha's laugh sounded far too near hysterics. Was this the true reason Ferox had called her across the mountains? Had she been led like a lamb to slaughter in the way Wolfsbane warned? And yet Grendel practically begged her to leave hours ago.

"I'm sorry to tell you I'm not anyone's savior, just another hedge witch," she insisted.

Hvalla only smiled and lifted her hand, again with seemingly great effort, until it brushed against the scarlet petals. "Tend your roses, mistress, and watch them grow. The blood will tell."

After dinner in the hall, Ferox presented a stack of thick and glistening tomes set on the table before the hearth. He smiled as Vynasha ran careful fingertips over gilded covers and hand-painted letters.

"They're so beautiful," she whispered into that hall, the silence broken only by the crackling hearth and Ferox's steady, billowing breaths.

"Indeed. Would you like to learn to read them?"

Hvalla believed Vynasha was the one to end their curse, but Ferox had said nothing of prophecy.

Unless he can't, because of the curse...

She lifted her gaze and didn't see the fierce teeth made for rending flesh, only her friend, Grendel's warnings be damned.

The dark thoughts lingered at the back of her mind, yet she forced a smile and said, "I know a little. Could you help with the rest?"

Ferox sank onto the rug beside her, watchful over her shoulder as she slowly read aloud.

As he aided her through a tale of the lands long before the curse, Vynasha decided she could ask after Ceddrych another night.

And when Ferox's furred hand pointed to certain words, Vynasha covered his hand with hers, savoring the warmth and safety he gave her.

She did not see the way Ferox struggled to breathe or the way his other hand dug divots into the rug beneath them.

It went on like this over the following peaceful days. Visits to her garden, Hvalla often working at her side, singing songs in the old tongue.

After she broke her fast, either Ferox or Odym accompanied her to visit Dragos or explore the lower levels of the grand castle.

She was wandering one such hall bedecked with suits of armor of ages past, some glistening with metal that shone like starfire and some so black they seemed crafted from shadow.

Odym knew much about each, explaining what came from across the Veil and what was worn to which battle.

"They called him Vonwere, and he is why the lands beyond the Veil were not ravaged by a dark phurie before Soraya could enter our lands."

"Odym?" she interrupted as she was wont to do.

"Yes, Mistress?" He favored her with that smile she'd only ever seen on her brother before, that of fond exasperation.

Vynasha thought of Soraya's diary and gave voice to the question anyway. "Were you once a knight?"

Odym froze in place, his slightly hunched spine straightening as he stared at Vonwere's rune-etched armor. She thought he might not answer or speak in riddles like he did when the curse kept him silent. His answer came softer than a whisper, so she leaned in to hear, "I was, once upon a time."

"Is your armor displayed here too?" She ran her fingers over the grooved flesh of her wrist.

Odym scoffed. "I am a disgraced knight, and the king would never have added mine to this hallowed hall. No, I was never a particularly good knight. But I did my duty to my queen, and that is more than most could say before the end."

She thought she recalled reading something about death and duty. She wondered if Odym still loved his dead queen. "My brother, Ceddrych, was a soldier for a time. He never saw it as a great honor since it wasn't his choice to serve."

Odym turned to her with a kind smile and a gaze that looked past her into days of old. "And yet he did his duty."

"I suppose." Vynasha frowned at the steel displayed on the wall above the suits of armor. Her dagger pressed warm reassurance against her stocking-clad thigh. "I wonder how much of a choice any of us has in the end. So few break from the mold we are forced into."

I should know, she thought. What future could she ever have in Whistleande as the village witch?

Odym hummed and then said, "Mayhap you will grow into something new here, Mistress?"

Vynasha laughed. Not even Grendel's magick could erase her scars. "If Ferox has his way, I'll be your mistress, in truth."

"No," Odym replied with a gentle press of his ghostly hand to hers. "You will be a queen."

"Please tell me you aren't trying to give me a crown," Vynasha later begged a startled Ferox. For once, she came upon him in the gardens. She was surprised to find him standing before her roses, a single, black-stemmed bud in his hand.

Though his hackles rose at the unexpected intrusion, Ferox turned to her with an amused tilt of his wolf-like head. "I thought your future title went without saying."

Vynasha crossed her arms over her chest. "You never said anything about *ruling* alongside you as queen. I just assumed you needed me to break your curse." She held her breath and silently prayed she hadn't gone too far.

Ferox's step brought him so near she could smell the forest and winter of his scent mix with the magick of her roses. He carefully placed the bud behind her ear. "And if I said I wanted you for more than breaking curses?"

Vynasha narrowed her eyes at the beastly prince but couldn't mask the tremor behind her words. "Have you found my brother yet?"

Ferox leaned back, and the sunlight made his golden horns gleam. "The Wylderlands are vast, Beauty, but we have his trail. It is only a matter of time. And now, would you care to venture about the grounds?"

Vynasha allowed him to change the subject and chose to believe his word. She had already said more than she should. Instead, she followed his lead, willing to give him the chance to prove his word. She let him convince her to take Dragos for a ride, and he loped alongside Vynasha on horseback, easily keeping pace with her horse's strides.

And as they dined later that evening, as the days passed with an ease she felt increasingly guilty for, Vynasha would beg the question, "Are you any closer to finding Ceddrych?"

And Ferox would reply, "Soon."

She wanted, no, *needed* to believe him. The rosebud he had plucked she kept upon her fireplace mantel. Each morning, she breathed in the fragrance with the beastly prince's promise in her heart. And yet...

Lyttia and Myrel whispered of the closeness between their master and new mistress. They spoke of hopes and dreams that made the pit in Vynasha's stomach grow ever greater.

"When this is over, we can see if our home still stands."

"Will the others come back to themselves?"

"Hush, Myrel! Do you wish to fade so quickly?"

"Forgive me, Lyttia."

Lying in her bed each morning and night, she wondered if Wyll was sleeping on the frozen ground or up against a tree. She could only hope and pray Wolfsbane and his daughter kept her nephew safe. She needed to believe her comfort was a small price to pay. Once she had Ceddrych back, it would have all meant something. And then Wyll would have a home and comforts she was coming to love.

"Love is a luxury you cannot afford," the walls whispered, but Vynasha did not want to listen.

CHAPTER SEVENTEEN

A Game of Fate

IN THE RARE hours she had to herself, Vynasha listened to howling beasts and moaning winds beating against the glass. Alone, she could pry Soraya's account from its new hiding place underneath the wardrobe. She read more of the intimacies between Soraya and Odym with a permanent blush.

Love and duty indeed.

Vynasha had never had time to hunt after a husband like her sisters had. Chores on the farm needed doing, and someone had to make sure Old Ced didn't harm himself while they weren't looking. His spirits had been dampened until the winter Ceddrych came home from the war. After the fire, she'd had her and little Wyll's lives to think on. It had been so long since she'd cared enough to think of her future, and love meant nothing to her. Love meant losing the ones dearest to her heart and the pain of missing them afterward. Loving someone was like passing on a death sentence, and Vynasha had not allowed herself to grow close to anyone in case she truly was cursed.

Hvalla's transparent features and her words crossed her memory then. "…*She made a promise that one day, one who possessed all of the blood would revoke the curse and mend the mirror.*"

Vynasha's hand hovered just above the inked-in text, over a word she recognized, which sent chills through her bones.

Mirror.

Odym had also spoken of the mirror between this world and the other, where Soraya had come from. She read on.

Odym has stolen the key to the mirror for me, though I fear the king already knows of his betrayal. It shall have to be enough for now. We cannot risk the king making use of it. Already, the sickness has filled his body and should claim him within the fortnight. If only Odym could convince our son to speak with me. If I could only talk with him about the things he saw on the other side of the mirror. I fear what will happen to him once my wrath has been unleashed. I cannot take back what has already been set in motion. Much as I try to tell myself he is no longer my son, Odym reminds me otherwise.

It is too late to return to my homeland, but mayhap she can mend it when she comes. I have seen her only in shadows of my dreams, but already, I can see she is going to be stronger than…

Vynasha shut the cover of the diary and gathered her knees under her chin. She shook her head, convinced she must be dreaming or mad.

It's not me.

But she had seen the arch that night on the balcony before the beast had chased her over the ledge and then saved her life. Magick more powerful than any she had felt before had given her the strength to call the wind to her fingertips.

The key.

Vynasha shivered as she pulled the strange twig-like object

from the back of the diary and wrapped her fingers around wood stronger than stone. "Is this ironbark?" she murmured aloud. Wynyth had spoken of ironbark in her stories, wood that not even steel could break.

The tapestry rippled with a hiss of air and a whispering voice warning, "*Careful, Beauty…*"

Vynasha slipped the key between her breasts inside her corset and winced as it scratched her skin. She brought another of Ferox's books to cover Soraya's diary just before Grendel slipped from the shadows.

The gatekeeper's visits had been inconstant, though usually after Odym had left Vynasha to her own devices.

"What do you want?" She opened the ancient tome lying atop Soraya's account and prayed the gatekeeper didn't look too closely.

"One of the black stems," Grendel muttered as he came limping to lean against the fireplace mantel and touched the rosebud she had left days before. "These were my mother's favorite flower, you know."

"Please leave my rose alone and go back to your beasts. I don't care to argue with you today, and I'm busy, as you can see." Vynasha returned her attention to the beautifully illustrated pages. A folktale, Ferox had called this one, though the image of wylderfolk in battle and illicit passions was far graver than any children's story she had known.

"You are idle, studying words in a dying language in a city of the dead," he said.

Vynasha rolled her eyes. "And yet you are, unfortunately, still breathing."

Grendel's pained laugh was so unexpected, Vynasha picked up her head and almost forgot the key between her breasts. The smile nearly split the gatekeeper's face in two and twisted his ever-scowling face into something far too beautiful to be human.

Damn him.

She turned another page, though she wasn't quite able to tear her gaze from his. "Shouldn't you be in the dungeons, keeping a leash on your beasts?"

His smile lingered. "My beasts are bound below the grounds, but I am not."

Vynasha traced a finger over the gossamer illustration of a lady's wing. "And yet one of your creatures chased me to the castle gates and later attacked me within these walls."

"That one is different." Grendel's scowl returned, and Vynasha found she could breathe far easier at the familiar sight.

"So you admit you have exceptions, then? I wonder how Ferox tolerates your mistakes."

"Please allow me to enjoy your fire in peace, would you, witch?" Grendel groaned, clutching his side as he sank onto the rug before her. His hand came away bloody, a deep indigo blue.

Vynasha left her book open over Soraya's diary. "You're bleeding."

"I am fine," he insisted, but she had already stood and rushed for the washbasin.

"Remove your clothes so I can see," she snapped as she wet a clean rag.

Grendel brushed her hands aside. "I do not need any of your bleeding mothering!"

Vynasha clenched her teeth together to keep the urge to slap him at bay as she met his eye. "I can promise you whatever it is, I've seen and tended to worse. Now either you strip, or I cut your clothes myself. Don't think I won't, gatekeeper."

The silence grew thick between them as Grendel held her glare. His jaw worked, and she narrowed her eyes, slipping her free hand to hike up her skirt.

Grendel's eye tracked the movement and widened before he

turned his head sharply away. "I cannot remove the coat alone."

Vynasha bit back her grin as she set upon the buttons and slowly peeled the coat over his shoulders. Grendel hissed as the fabric stuck to the wounds. The tattered shirt was soaked.

"Did you have trouble with one of the beasts?" she said to ease the tension as she pulled her dagger from under her skirts and cut his shirt away from his back. Every rip and tear seemed louder to her ears than it should, and she was not prepared for the claw marks the fabric unveiled.

A dark eyebrow arched when she knelt beside him to further inspect the damage. "Why do you look so shocked, witch? I do bleed when injured," he scoffed. "I may not be frail as a human, but I am not immune."

She bit her lip as she studied the deep teeth marks in his hand and said, "It's amazing you haven't been eaten yet." She tore strips of fabric from her skirt and dipped them in the nearby basin before returning to catch the scratches on his neck.

"Mayhap the beasts would listen better to you."

"Was your head addled as well?" She set the soiled scraps to join his ruined shirt.

He shook his head and tilted it back with a bitter laugh. "I must tell you now, I suppose. You cannot marry *him* without knowing."

"Knowing what?" She tore more wool fabric from her skirt with a sigh. "You and Ferox have a terrible habit of pretending I already have the answers." He flinched when she steadied his head with a firm grip on his jaw and pressed her thumb into the slight cut on his neck. She was surprised to feel so many unnoticeable scars beneath her touch.

"We are cursed, Vynasha, and none can speak the truth to you without consequences. But I cannot watch you wither away like this in silence any longer."

A shiver laced her spine. "Wither away? I feel stronger here than I have in…"

Forever.

He leaned forward and clenched his fists, growling out impatiently, "That is the magick in our blood keeping the worst at bay. But if you choose to stay, you *will* be cursed like the rest of us. Our queen fashioned the curse to prevent all from going through the mirror into her world. Blood is the only thing that can cleanse us and the only price *she* will accept."

"You speak as if Soraya were still alive," she said then gasped as Grendel covered her mouth with his hand. His violet-gray eyes darted about the room. Her fingers found his wrist, and she flinched at his proximity.

Grendel's gaze flickered as her mouth parted against his palm. He pulled away carefully, and his brow creased. "Never speak her name aloud, not unless you want to draw her attention." At Vynasha's confused frown, he continued, "All the cursed souls that have faded never left. They linger in the walls, in the tapestries, in the very foundations beneath us. With each soul that fades, the curse grows in strength. If you were not who we think you are, you would never have been able to pass through the enchanted forest. And did you not wonder why your blood made the roses bloom?"

"How do you know that?" she asked in fear.

He grabbed her hand before she could pull away. "I already told you," he said between clenched teeth as he easily pressed her palm against his neck.

"Let go." Her hand spasmed against his neck.

A feverish light burned within his eyes along with the press of his magick rising between them. "Are you truly so ignorant of your own power? Your potential? You could cleanse all things, cleanse even me, if you wanted."

"Let go of me!" She reached blindly beside her for the blade she had foolishly discarded and nicked her fingers with a curse.

"If you would only listen! Stop fighting me, witch," he growled back.

But before she could turn her blade on him, the claw marks in his chest and neck began to fade before her eyes. The blood seeping from the sealing wounds gleamed a brilliant violet. Vynasha hissed as Grendel caught her other wrist, squeezing until she released her dagger.

He pulled her hands away and between them with wonder. "Your blood, my blood…"

"Our blood," she whispered, crimson and blue turning to violet blood coating her fingers. "What… what have you done to me?"

"This was your doing, witch, can you not see? They were wrong about you. You are so much more than any of them could want, even more than she predicted."

Air caught in her lungs, unable to escape her chest. Not when he reached up to clasp her face. His form did not glow as brightly as before, and his gray skin darkened further as he asked, "What are you?"

She shook her head in his hold. "I don't know anymore."

Grendel's thumb brushed over her mouth, and she sucked in a sharp breath. She didn't hate the gatekeeper, but she didn't like him, either. And yet…

"If I let you do this, there's the chance she could possess you, ruin you," he murmured to himself. "And I am not willing to let her have you, to let *any* other have you."

The trail he made with his thumbs over her nose and the lines of her jaw, the way his eyes followed his touch, like he was seeing her for the first time. Tears spilled from her eyes as he purposely touched the mottled skin of her cheek.

"Please stop," she begged, her voice falling into a low rasp. "Stop looking at me like that."

"Like what?" A gentle reverence smoothed his features, and all his bitter masks seemed to fade away.

For one completely mad moment, Vynasha longed to return his touch in kind. She wanted to run her fingers over the bare scrap of beard clinging to his jaw, to urge his expressive mouth into that devastating smile.

A distant roar broke out, shattering through her madness. The creature was too far away to threaten them just yet but still much closer than it should be.

Vynasha pulled free of Grendel's hold and stumbled to her feet. Grendel quickly followed, muttering in the old tongue as he reached for his soiled coat. The muscles in his lean torso shifted as he slipped the filthy garment over his bare chest. Her heart raced too quickly still, and the air still smelled too strongly of magick and roses.

The beast roared again, closer this time. She sucked in a breath as something tugged deep within her chest, and she wondered if the cry came from her beast.

"I have to go." Grendel had moved so quickly she was surprised to find him striding back from the secret passage. He pulled a velveteen pouch from his coat pocket. "Take this. It will guard you from *her* sight."

"What is it?"

"Protection and more." His gaze softened a shade, then he added, "Speak to it, and it will tell you things you wish to remember. Then dream and remember me."

"Thank you," she replied. "For keeping me safe and risking the curse."

"If you wish to truly thank me, Vynasha, you'll climb onto your horse and ride as far and fast from this place as you can. And you will not look back."

CHAPTER EIGHTEEN

A Spark of Prophecy

A KNOCK CAME AT her door, long after the flames dwindled from a roaring yellow to pale blue. Vynasha cursed under her breath as she threw the silver-chained amulet around her neck and hid it beneath her shift. "Bloody enchantments."

How long had she been lost to Grendel's gift and the thoughts tumbling madly through her head?

For not the first time, Vynasha wished her mother were still alive. If the fever hadn't taken Wynyth and she hadn't wasted away, would she have warned Vynasha about curses and blood magick? All she had to guide her were half-remembered tales from her childhood and all she had gleaned through Ceddrych's books.

Vynasha had been stupid to leave the bloody dagger and Soraya's diary in the open as she did. "Mistakes get you killed," she muttered as she gathered the diary and shoved it beneath her pillow. The blade she returned to the makeshift sheath she often tied to her hip.

Another, louder knock, followed by Odym's call. "Mistress?

Might I enter?"

She hesitated as the amulet pulsed with sudden heat against her bare skin, and she resisted the urge to pry it free and chuck it into the flames. But far better to keep Grendel's gift on her person than risk the maids finding it. At least Odym had purposely left her the diary.

The door slowly creaked open. "Mistress? Are you awake?"

Vynasha stuffed the pouch after the diary and ran a hand through her curls. Grendel wanted her gone for good, but she wasn't about to condemn the ones left behind to Soraya's dark vengeance. No matter the risk to herself.

"I'm here," she called as she left her bedside and met Odym at her door.

The old knight nearly floated into the room, his pale gaze sweeping over her with concern. "I was sent to help prepare you for supper. Master bid me tell you he has a surprise in store for you."

Vynasha allowed herself to be led to the wardrobe, where she watched as Odym removed a shimmering golden gown with voluptuous skirts from deep within. "What is that?"

Odym arched an eyebrow at her. "A gown, Mistress."

Vynasha shook her head. "Yes, I can see that. But it is far too fine for me." She ran her scarred hand over the amber-beaded bodice and thought of her dead sisters. "Not for me," she insisted.

Odym was silent a moment before setting the gown aside and whispering, "Lyttia and Myrel hoped you would like it. I believe they said amber was Master's favored precious stone. Shall I fetch you a cup of tea while you dress?"

Vynasha snorted. "Fine, you've shamed me into it. I'll wear the dress. And I'll drink the tea if you'll make a cup for yourself and add a hearty dose of spirits."

Odym's smile soothed the lingering ache in her blood from healing Grendel. "A sound plan, Mistress."

Vynasha waited until the door closed behind him before

meeting her gaze in the wardrobe mirror. The shadows under her eyes were not so pronounced, and her cheeks were fuller than they'd been upon her arrival. How long had she been here? It couldn't be more than a few weeks at the most. She looked taller, and her gray eyes gleamed silver.

She undressed slowly and grimaced at Grendel's blood still staining her fingertips. She had gotten rid of the evidence earlier, but his stain lingered. And with each beat of her heart, she wondered if Grendel was still infecting her, his magick warping and changing hers. The amulet glinted silver and amethyst against her chest.

"*What are you?*" he had asked, but Vynasha still didn't know.

She donned the bodice and skirts, lacing as much as she could, then tied Ferox's dagger to her thigh as she always did.

The clink of cups signaled Odym's return. She turned to watch Soraya's knight set the tray on her small dining table and prepare the cup just how she preferred. A smile tugged at her mouth to see him uncork a squat dark bottle and add a dusky-brown liquid to the tea.

Vynasha crossed the room and lifted the offered cup to her lips, waiting until Odym had finished his own before taking a sip. She grimaced at the sharp honey tang and sighed as it warmed her throat.

They stood together in a peace interrupted by a cacophony of howls in the chambers below. Was Grendel going to be okay?

"The beasts are restless tonight," Odym remarked.

Vynasha shivered as she drew another sip, Grendel's words heavy upon her. "Odym, I don't think I can do this. Everyone expects so much of me, but what if you're wrong? What if I'm not the one? What if I make things worse? How can I know if…"

If I'm making the right choice.

Because Ferox and Grendel had been right: she always had a choice. And she wasn't sure if either would lead to the ending she dreamed of.

When did you forget life is not a fairy tale?

Odym watched her for a long moment as though reading the unspoken thoughts upon her face. Finally, he sighed and said, "Tell me, what have you learned from *her* letters?"

Vynasha's brow drew together, and she tapped a broken fingernail on the glass. "You know about the diary?"

His smile grew as he confessed. "I left her account where you would be most likely to find it."

Vynasha laughed. "In that case, I've almost finished."

Odym nodded, and his features faded into his usual solemn mask. "And so you know."

"I know she hated the king in the end for turning their son against her. That she resorted to dark magick and placed her curse, knowing it would eventually consume her too." Vynasha swallowed the last of her tea and set the cup down. "And you arranged to be her personal guard. You told the king that he should only trust you with the task."

A corner of Odym's sagging cheeks lifted, and his eyes lit with memory. "Ah, yes… how foolish of him, would you not agree?"

"You made plans to run away together, but your master knew you were his mother's lover," she continued as Odym came around to finish tying her laces. "The king had their son alter the spell so she couldn't escape her room. And he did this to punish you both, he told her. That was the last time she saw her child."

Odym inhaled sharply and pressed his hands to her shoulders, his voice a pained whisper. "The kingdom beyond the Veil demanded the king release their princess. The folk of air wanted her to return and take her mother's throne. When the king refused, war was made between our worlds. Beofric threatened to use the mirror's magick to attack them."

He trailed off, and Vynasha turned to find him staring at the door. The howling of beasts echoed deep within the castle. Had Grendel managed to subdue them without bloodshed this time?

"You broke the mirror so no one could escape or return from the other side," she said. "To prevent the war."

Odym's form rippled before he tore his attention from the door and back to her. "And yet we still lost everything. *She* is faded, along with so many of my kin."

Faded but not dead?

Before Vynasha gathered the courage to ask, Odym continued, "The rest that have not lingered became the monsters they once feared and dreamed of. My prince kept order for a time, even sought for ways to break his mother's curse, but the darkness grows ever stronger."

"If the mirror is broken, it can't be used to harm anyone now, right?" she asked as she followed Odym into the hallway beyond her room.

He spoke softly, gaze sharp on the listening shadows of the castle corridors. "It may still be used to peer beyond our borders or within. Yet my queen claimed there was a way to return it to its original purpose. I wish I knew how."

Vynasha shook her head. "But you risked so much to destroy it."

Odym sighed, the weight of nearly three centuries within his reply. "I should like to see the place we vowed to escape to at least once before I die."

Vynasha hesitated before catching Odym's hand in hers. "If I'm everything they say, I swear you will."

His eyes gleamed brighter for a moment, and his smile stretched across his face in a way that showed her how he might have once looked in his youth. He covered her hand with one of his own before guiding it to his elbow. "Mayhap," he finally said as he guided her along.

"So, is this why Grendel hates the prince so much? Because he helped create the beasts?"

"Grendel?" Odym exclaimed.

"We… He has aided me before and visits from time to time,"

she confessed, wondering if it was wise to say so.

"I trust you haven't been venturing to those awful dungeons on your own." His wide, luminous gaze narrowed with suspicion.

"Not exactly," she said, making a face. "I had an unfortunate encounter with one of his beasts, and Grendel protected me. He's not as pleasant as you or Ferox, but… he said some things to me about the curse and your master. I can't help but wonder if he's right."

When the old knight gave no reply, she lifted her eyes to search his face. He seemed to hold something back with a sheer force of will, but in the end, he only nodded with a sigh and hunched further.

"Any questions you have, you should ask Master Ferox," he said. "But I beg of you, do not mention Grendel to him. In fact, it is best if you do not speak his name too loudly beyond your room."

Vynasha opened her mouth, but Odym paused, and she realized they were already standing before the doors to the dining hall.

"Master is already waiting. I do hope you enjoy your gift, Mistress," he said before squeezing her hand and pulling away.

Vynasha nodded to him and drew in a steadying breath as she reached for the door handle. She clenched her fist to keep it from trembling and then noticed the dried violet blood flecks on her hands. She had forgotten to wash them.

Cursing under her breath, Vynasha carefully lifted her golden skirts and attempted to scrub the stain from her hands. Dread settled like a weight in her stomach as she wondered if he would be able to smell the blood anyway.

As before, the door swung open with a silence she was used to by now. She glanced up at the hunting trophies displayed above the symbols and crests on the wall. Highest above sat the massive dragon skulls, half a house wide, betraying but a hint of their former might.

The long table was already set with the delicious food the hidden staff had prepared for them. Past this stood the hearth, and just above it, the castle banner hung. Letters too archaic for her to recognize spelled a short phrase beneath a faded coat of arms. Its symbol looked like a pair of bat wings wrapping around a cluster of stars. Twin claws reached from underneath to bar in warning, and the silver thread caught stray casts of candlelight.

The heavy carpet softened her tread, so the rustling of skirts filled her ears instead. Ferox stood from the shelter of his high-backed chair at her approach. She would never grow used to how so hulking a being could move so gracefully.

"Beauty," Ferox greeted.

"Beast." She pushed aside her fears and forced herself to accept his outstretched palm, barely pressing her fingers into his paw as he escorted her to her seat. After tucking her into the table, he moved to his far larger chair, long since placed closer to her side.

"Tell me, how have you occupied your day? Did you read any of the books I leant you?"

The red contents in her glass nearly spilled over as she struggled to right it before downing a healthy dose. "Shit, sorry," she cursed aloud and panicked until Ferox's chuckle echoed through the spacious hall.

"I prefer an honest tongue in my future bride."

Vynasha concentrated on drinking without dropping her goblet. "You must consider me quite the prize, then."

Ferox smiled as he lifted a roasted leg of meat and took a bite with sharp teeth. It had taken several meals before he seemed comfortable enough to eat in front of her. Vynasha had grown so accustomed that she was startled to notice his beastly finesse. As ever, she was struck by the contradiction he posed, neither fully wild nor civilized but somewhere in between.

Vynasha did her best to eat and share her thoughts about the book she had pretended to read in front of Grendel earlier. If Ferox smelled the gatekeeper's blood on her skin or skirts, he gave no indication.

The food could be helping with this.

"I am pleased you have taken such an interest in Vonwere and Ynaea's tale," Ferox was saying.

Vynasha blinked and forced her focus on the beast she had promised herself to. "Odym showed me Vonwere's armor the other day."

"He found many occasions to wear that set, I believe. But he never hesitated to bring war to Ynaea's enemies. I often believed Vonwere and Ynaea should never have been bound together. For when he first found her, he thought her a myth, a being so powerful she should not have existed."

"And she thought him a beast?" Vynasha teased. "Vonwere's armor might easily fit you, Ferox."

He drank deeply from his cup and licked his lips, and something in the action made her breath quicken. "As it should. Vonwere was kin to me."

"Oh..." Vynasha rubbed her finger over the gold-gilded silverware. "It's so strange..."

Ferox placed a clawed hand close to hers. "Because he was real?"

Vynasha nodded and smiled. "For someone who claims not to read minds, you see my thoughts too well."

Ferox regarded her with the same longing she was coming to both savor and dread. "Come, I have something to show you, Beauty."

Vynasha allowed him to pull her from the table and outside the great hall. "Is this the surprise Odym told me about?" she teased, praying he couldn't feel the tremor in her limbs. Her bad leg seemed to suddenly ache, her scars tightening and the walls pressing against their path as they slowly ascended to the floor above.

Ferox's sharp teeth gleamed with his smile against the flickering candlelight. "I see my old friend has been spilling secrets." He gently squeezed her hand, and she hated the comfort she found in his hold.

Vynasha held his gaze, trusting his lead despite herself as they ascended yet another floor. "He's loyal to you."

They paused before a heavily ornate door, familiar figures carved into the wood she barely noticed before Ferox came to stand close before her.

"He is loyal to *you*, as he should be to his future queen," her Beast said with a low rumble.

Vynasha leaned into his warmth and forgot her fears entirely for a moment. She reached a hand to press against the white fur at his collar and, holding his gaze, carded her fingers through it.

Ferox's jaw snapped shut with an audible click as he shuddered then held still. His green gaze burned like twin emerald flames.

She bit her lip briefly as she took another step into his space and said, "I think… it may not be so terrible to be your queen."

His chest expanded and collapsed as his free hand caught the back of her amber-beaded dress. His claws were far too near the amulet Grendel had gifted her. Yet he seemed not to notice, as his nose pressed to the crux of her neck and her unbound curls. "I *will* make you my queen, and I will keep you safe, sacred from all others. My Beauty…"

Something hot and wet met her neck briefly over her scars. His tongue?

Vynasha bit back a moan as she clung tightly to his collar. The feeling rattled her bones, settled deeply to the root of her, and made her *want* for something she didn't know how to name. She tilted her head slightly, baring her neck even more.

Ferox growled deeply and drew her closer until she was forced to the tips of her toes, and he curled over her, the graze of sharp teeth scraping her bared skin.

The amulet at her neck pulsed, painfully hot, and Vynasha gasped, this time in pain.

Ferox released her so quickly she landed painfully on her bad leg. His chest rose and fell, and she looked up to find him suddenly leaning his head heavily against the door. "Forgive me," he rumbled. "I have no right to claim what you have not yet given me."

She pressed a palm over the amulet, which had instantly gone cold, and grimaced as her racing heart slowed. There were moments when she had wondered what it might be like to be Ferox's bride. She had never allowed herself to wonder if he would want her as he would a true mate, hadn't thought it possible. But now…

Vynasha swallowed back all the things she shouldn't say, the mad urge to tell him she would give everything Ferox asked. Though she barely understood the feelings lingering like magick buzzing beneath her skin, Grendel's amulet weighed heavily around her neck.

"I should have brought you here long ago," Ferox said before pulling open the door.

"What do you—" Vynasha gasped as a gust of frozen wind braced them. "Wait!" She reached blindly for Ferox and staggered after his retreat.

The ceiling rose high above them, so the flames burning from the hearth didn't quite reach the figures carved into the eaves. A beautiful, canopied bed sat against one wall, covered in gleaming tapestries. Candles glowed from every surface, at odds with the constant winter wind that pulled her curls back from her head, drying all traces of *his* beastly kiss from her scars.

"Wait…" she murmured as she followed Ferox to the stone arch at the center of the room.

I was here.

She froze as she took in the fully restored glass wall, the door open to the balcony, and the mended bed and furnishings.

The arch practically hummed as Ferox reached it and placed a clawed hand upon the runes. "I had planned to wait until after our bonding ceremony to present this as a gift to you, Beauty."

"The mirror," she whispered. Gooseflesh rose along her arms, pricking the back of her neck. Magick required sacrifice, and Vynasha lost much of what made her mortal by bringing Wyll back. And yet this arch, the *mirror* Soraya spoke of in her diary, in the light of this eve, apart from her terror of that other beast, made her skin crawl.

"Yes." Ferox's claws scraped the black stone as he twisted his head and his eye roved over her. "Will you not come closer, Beauty? I promised you power, as you will recall."

Vynasha's leg ached as her body tried to obey his call. His voice was soothing, the voice that had pulled her from dreams in time to save Wyll, that had kept her safe all the months after. Ferox was her friend, her prince, the one who would help her find Ceddrych. And when she found Ceddrych, they would bring Wyll to the castle and be a family again.

And Father too? A darker part of her bucked against unwanted memories, jerking her into the present.

Ferox crooked his hand, beckoning her. "Do you not wish to see your brother, Beauty? Come and use the mirror. Call to him as I called to you, and let us bring him home." His smile stretched across his wolfish face, a terribly beautiful smile.

Still, Vynasha couldn't seem to move no matter how much she longed to take his hand. "But you have already been searching for him, haven't you?"

Could he have used the mirror all along?

If she had not spent so many days studying the shifting tells in his green eyes, Vynasha would have missed the way his gaze fell flat.

"Ceddrych's visage has been clouded to me, but as kin, you will surely find him."

Vynasha stared at the rippling shimmer that passed over the arch. "I don't know… I should wait, shouldn't I? If our marriage will undo the curse, then I should wait."

"Wait?" Ferox's claws dug deeper into the stone mirror, and a hard edge twisted his sharp smile.

Vynasha met his gaze and dug her nails into her palms. "Yes, *wait.*"

Ferox chuffed. "I offer you power none other has been offered, and you choose to wait?"

Vynasha shivered as the mirror pulsed and the space within the arch flickered. Again, the sense of wrongness kept Vynasha rooted to the spot, and her anger rose with Ferox's patronizing tone. "The room is beautiful, and the offer is most generous, Beast, but I'm not going anywhere near your cursed mirror."

"I have never thought you to be a fool, Vynasha," Ferox growled. "Yet I suppose it was too much to hope for a woman so young to fully understand."

"I may be young, but I'm not an *idiot*, Ferox!" Vynasha pulled back her hair to reveal the scars trailing down her face and neck. "I know all magick requires sacrifice. Can you promise me that thing won't lash out at me if I dare touch it?"

"Not so long as I am here with you," he countered.

"I don't believe you." Vynasha laughed. "You know what I do believe? I believe *you* don't understand the power you're trying to wield. And why do you need me to do this so badly?"

"You know I cannot tell you! You know I am bound by this bloody mirror, but if you claim control, you can put an end to all of this."

Vynasha took a step back. "Bring Ceddrych to me. Bring my brother home, and I'll marry you and do whatever else you tell me."

The weight in her heart lifted with hope as they stood opposed before the mirror. Hope that the beastly prince would say yes and honor his word. Her hand twitched as she resisted the urge to reach for him. Maybe he was right?

"Say it," she rasped, shoes scraping as she dared a step forward. "Say you will."

"Vynasha…"

"Say you haven't lied to me from the very beginning. That you haven't made me a fool. *Make* me trust you, Ferox, please. Give me a reason!"

Ferox growled low as he turned his wolfish profile to her. "I cannot…"

Vynasha pressed a palm against her chest, over the burn of stone on scarred skin. She blinked back tears. "You can't or won't?"

Ferox's growl deepened as he released the mirror and stalked to her. "This bickering is pointless when you may see the truth with your touch."

"What are you doing?" Vynasha stumbled out of his reach, and her bad leg refused to catch her. "Ferox, wait," she begged.

He caught her arm and dragged her back to the arch, ignoring her pained cries. "I should have done this from the beginning, as she told me to," he groaned in anguish, tears darkening the fur about his eyes.

"No!" She jerked in his hold as he wrapped himself around her, lifting her arms like a puppeteer. "Stop! You're going to kill us all if you don't stop," she moaned as weakness filled her limbs.

The heat in her blood, that thrum of power that the castle and its beast and roses had awoken, failed her.

The dagger was beyond her reach, and her sobs fell on deaf ears as she bucked against Ferox's hold.

Saints above, he's too strong!

As their connected limbs reached for the stone arch, the runes flared with violet light.

Ferox stilled, and Vynasha gasped for breath to beg, "Please don't, please don't make me…"

I might have loved you. I might have stayed forever if you did as you promised.

"Our fate would always have led us to this." His horned helm brushed the top of her head, and then his nose pressed desperately to her neck. "Forgive me, Beauty."

Vynasha's lips parted in a silent scream as Ferox forced her to touch the mirror.

The light from the runes flared and blinded her, scouring and following her closed eyelids. Her body jerked against an impossibly firm hold as fire licked through her arms and tears of blood spilled past her closed eyelids.

Ferox said she would understand, that she would *see*.

All she felt was the pain of an ancient power shattered into pieces she couldn't begin to put together.

But the worst pain of all came from the betrayal of the one she was learning to love.

His words and actions cut the threads which had bound them so tightly. Months of his voice in her head, of his voice keeping her alive and sound of mind.

All she saw was unending violet light breaking over her in waves and consuming her until her heart cleaved in two.

CHAPTER NINETEEN

A Grim Betrayal

"BEAUTY," THE VOICE called to her over mountains and forests and river valleys. The voice had been with her through flame and frost, tragedy and terror.

"Beauty, are you awake?"

Beast?

Vynasha opened her eyes to blackness and the persistent drip of the dungeons. As feeling crept back into her body, she groaned at the assault of fresh aches and pricks needling her skin. She ran her fingers over her hands to find them scarred and gleaming with fresh welts.

Ferox, she thought as visions of his pained emerald eyes surfaced. She squeezed her eyes shut and took in a much-needed breath as she sat up. She wished she could scrape the images from her mind, the sting of betrayal.

He lied, just as Grendel said he would.

She clenched her fists and wished she were somewhere

far away and safe with Wyll. "I never should have left you," she whispered, swallowing lingering traces of blood in her mouth. She wiped the corner of her mouth then froze. The blood on her finger glowed iridescent violet, the same as Grendel's.

"Beauty?" The voice from her nightmares echoed in the dungeon walls.

"Beast?" Vynasha staggered to her feet with a pained groan and shuffled to the door of her cell. She reached up on the balls of her feet and peered through the window of bars into the dimly lit passage.

The beastly prince's curling horned headdress and large indigo cloak masked much of his white-furred form. His once-kind green eyes burned with some unnamed emotion. A day ago, Vynasha would have guessed his mood; now, she questioned ever knowing him in truth. She hated the comfort she found at the sight of him.

"Why am I here, Ferox?" She wrapped her fingers around the crude bars.

His gaze settled on the luminous blood staining her hand, and his nostrils flared. "How can you ask me that? When we are here because of what *you* have done."

"What I did?" Vynasha choked back a sob. "I trusted you, and you betrayed me!"

"I betrayed you?" Ferox leaned forward and sniffed at her bloodied hand, and his lip curled over too-sharp teeth. "I believed you were the one to break the curse. After watching you for months from afar, I felt I knew you as well as my own flesh. And now…"

Vynasha's limbs shook, but she refused to flinch as he growled and dug his claws into the wooden door above her bars. "I never asked for this, Ferox," she managed, but her words passed between them faintly.

"You were our last hope and my salvation. I could not understand what you had done, why the mirror rejected you so." Ferox's clawed hand hovered briefly over the bars between them before his pained gaze hardened into stone. "Until your *bonded* appeared in a mad rage and nearly destroyed everything."

Vynasha shook her head. "Bonded?"

"*Grendel* has already stolen everything I loved in his arrogance." Ferox took a staggering step back and growled, "And now, because you have polluted yourself, I am forced, yet again, to watch a maid I love become a monster."

Vynasha sucked in a sharp breath at the finality in his tone. The bars tore at her tender hands as she pulled her weight up on them to cry out. "Ferox, wait! Don't leave me here alone. By all the saints, I swear I didn't know."

Ferox continued to walk away, yet his words carried, danced against the dungeon corridor. "A pity you could not love a beast."

"Wait!" she sobbed when Ferox melded into darkness. "Please don't leave me here!"

Only the distant snarls and bellows of other prisoners answered her pleas. She grabbed at her chest, where the amulet rested, at the emptiness clawing her belly, and turned to face her tomb. Her skin began to glow the same violet as her blood as she sank onto the floor and hid her tears in her hands.

While the other beasts in this dank prison howled and time crawled, Vynasha watched the way her inner violet light glowed beneath her skin. Scant incandescence, not enough to breach the black surrounding her.

"I didn't know," she whispered. "I swear, I didn't know, Wyll."

She closed her eyes and saw the scars covering half of Wyll's sweet face, the brightness in his blue eyes as she'd passed him off to Wolfsbane for safekeeping. The journey she'd made into the castle would have been too dangerous for her to carry him along. So she'd braved the terror of the unnatural wolves as they gave chase up to the castle gates. She could still see the giant doors and remembered her crippling loss of hope upon entering. Her skin still prickled at the memory of that first awful night, when the beast appeared, snarling and clawing after her flesh. It was impossible to fathom how much her perception of the castle's mysterious inhabitants would change in one season. They had unwittingly influenced her, especially Ferox, with his boundless knowledge of places and things she only dreamed of.

Would it have been so terrible to love him if he'd only let me?

"*Vynasha,*" the walls called to her in a harsh whisper.

She opened her eyes and cursed. "Leave me alone. I'm through with listening to you, Soraya."

"Do not speak her name. You have done enough to draw her ire."

"Grendel?" Vynasha managed through a sudden rush of tears. "I thought I was alone."

"Our *master* placed me in the cell beside yours. Come toward my voice if you can."

"Where?"

"Here."

She tripped over her voluminous skirts as the stones to her right shifted and spilled onto the floor. Dim blue light spilled through the hole in the lower portion of the wall. "Oh, Saints, you might have warned me," she grumbled.

"Forgive me for not accommodating you," came his wavering reply, far weaker than before.

Vynasha crawled until she could peer through the hole Grendel had made. The chains binding him scraped the wall she peered through, yet only his shoulders and profile were visible. She pushed her hand into the hole until her fingertips brushed his shoulder. "Are you well?"

"I am chained to a damned wall," he grumbled, but he leaned into her touch.

Vynasha pressed her forehead against the dungeon wall and sighed. "I don't remember what happened after touching the mirror, but after what Ferox said… thank you."

"For what?" Grendel's harsh tone couldn't hide the way he

twisted against his chains to see her.

"For trying to save me." Vynasha shut her eyes and pressed her cheek to the chilled stone. "I'm glad you came for me," she confessed and then after a pause added, "Grendel, why did Ferox call you my bonded?"

"The blood will tell," he muttered.

"Grendel, how bad are your injuries? I cannot believe you would try to fight Ferox."

He laughed again mirthlessly. "Your beast fought far better than expected for an old dog. Yet he might have finished me off were it not for you."

"What do you mean?"

Grendel groaned as he shifted away from her touch and turned his face away. "You already know the answer, Vynasha."

"How can I…" Vynasha dug her fingers into the broken rock and recalled the moment she'd healed his wounds without effort, a joining of her blood with his. Dread filled her like a weight in the pit of her stomach. "We healed each other."

And created a blood bond… Saints, I'm such a fool.

"You spoke in your dreams. That was what drew me to you from the beginning. I knew from the moment you crossed our threshold you were special, but after I found your things and read Ceddrych's letters, I needed to know you as he did."

"Wait, *you* stole my pack? Where is it?" Vynasha's skin brightened as she reached for his shoulder again, ignoring the way the stone scratched her cheek as she growled. "Grendel, look at me!"

His profile twisted toward her as though against his will. "Forgive me. I did not mean to form a bond with you at first. But from the moment my claw first grazed you and I truly *saw* you, I knew I could not fight it for long."

"Your claw?" She almost growled in frustration when he answered with silence. "Speak sense, you mad bastard. At least tell me my brother's letters are safe, or I swear on Wynyth's name I will haunt you far worse than *Soraya* ever could."

Vynasha strained to keep hold of him as Grendel pulled free from her reach and slipped away with a sharp breath. This was her only warning before the door to her cell creaked open behind her with a groan. She nearly ripped a fresh hole in her arm as she tried to wrench it from the hole Grendel had made between their cells.

For one torturous moment, she envisioned Ferox's gravelly voice and shadowed horns. Judging by their last conversation, she knew he would not want her speaking to Grendel, or anyone for that matter.

Vynasha scrambled to her feet, an arduous task thanks to the awkward position she had been lying in. Her skirts dragged on the filthy floor as she clung to the shadows then froze as the door opened and pale-blue light spilled into the cell.

"Odym! What are you doing here?"

Her first friend in the castle froze in wide-eyed horror at the sight of her. "Careful, Mistress." Odym glanced back over his shoulders. He opened the cloth bundle in his hands and urged, "Quickly, you must eat."

She wasted no time digging into the bread and cheese he had brought. "Glad as I am to see you, you shouldn't have risked it."

Odym shook his head and glanced back over his shoulder again at the echo of beastly groans. "We are under orders not to visit you, but Lyttia would not let you starve. I could not steal away until now. *He* is sleeping."

"You mean Ferox," she whispered as she clutched half of the bundle to her chest. It was clear then that the castle's ruler intended for her to suffer and fade too, like the wylderfolk, like the magick of this place. The knowledge filled her chest with an indefinable ache.

Odym wrung his hands and snuck glances back at the open cell door, anywhere but at her, and this made her more afraid than anything.

She took in his overall haggard appearance and placed a hand on his shoulder. "Odym, what did he say to you?"

His voice was bleak, hollow. "You are to be treated as the others who came before you, to wait and see whether you wither or are transformed. Yet we could not bear to abandon you, not when you do not know the truth."

"Odym," Grendel growled through the rocks in warning.

Odym turned with suspicion then crept over to the small opening amid the rubble. "Foolish boy, what are you about, locking yourself in there? Is this why the master is keeping stricter watch on the upper levels? I had wondered why the other beasts were so restless of late."

Vynasha took Odym by the arm before Grendel could reply and forced him to face her. "What do you mean, transformed?" She dug her nails into her palm to quell her panic. Down here in the bowels of Grendel's nightmare domain, transformation could only mean one thing.

"Leave her be, you meddling old fool!" Grendel shouted through their shared wall.

Odym lifted an eyebrow at the wall and then turned his questioning look to her. Vynasha sighed and spoke on her fellow inmate's behalf. "He hurt himself trying to save me from the mirror."

"He—what?" Odym stuttered, glancing from her to the gap in the stone. "Grendel, my boy, what have you done? Please tell me this madness is not your doing."

"Curse the both of you," Grendel grumbled.

"Odym, please," she said, clutching his lace cuffs. "If I'm going to die, I want to know the truth."

Odym's fingers trembled as he wrapped her hand in his, a look of pity in his faded eyes. "Master believed you would bring an end to this madness, but we knew in ways he could not that you are also *our* last hope."

"You go too far, old man," Grendel interrupted.

Odym did not acknowledge the gatekeeper but squeezed her hand. "Grendel and I are tied to the magick of this place, and as the wards have faded, so, too, have we. But if you succeed where others have failed, you might be the key to end our torment."

"You cannot ask this of her! You have no right!" Grendel struggled against the rocks.

Vynasha couldn't look away from the quiet hope in Odym's eyes as she said, "I thought marrying Ferox would end the curse."

"Ferox wanted your aid in controlling the mirror with your magick. But no marriage to that one would end the curse."

"Enough!" The rock wall shifted as Grendel pulled at his chains. "Vynasha, do not listen to this mad fool, I beg of you."

Despite Grendel's protests, she could not peel her eyes from Odym's. "Why are you telling me this now? Why not before?"

Odym bowed his head. "At first, we could not be certain. And then…I wondered if it would be better for all if you bonded with Ferox." He turned to glare at the wall as he added, "Until Grendel took matters into his own hands and bound you to himself first."

The wall shuddered with the force of Grendel's desperation, and his cries turned to the old tongue, to harsh words whose meaning she could only guess.

Vynasha released Odym's hands to hide the sudden snap of magick burning beneath her skin. "You should have spoken sooner," she hissed. "Maybe then, I wouldn't have become bound to *him* and left to rot in this cell." She gestured to the muck and the damp filth around them, furiously blinking back tears. "I can't trust any of you, but I don't have a choice anymore. Tell me what I need to do to transform and not fade like you."

Odym turned to look over his shoulder and then at the wall as it shuddered one last time and sighed. "It has already begun, from the moment you crossed our threshold and the old magick awoke within your blood. Ferox forced it further by attempting to bind you to the mirror, but truly, the greatest trial is still to come. If you stay here, if you let the magick of this prison transform you like it did the others, you may lose yourself. I cannot tell you what way the curse will manifest in you. But if you are truly of the blood, you will endure and save us all."

Grendel's horror drowned out the old man's words. "She cannot do this! No one has retained their true self in this place, old fool."

Vynasha looked to the hole and growled, "You don't get to dictate what I can and can't do, gatekeeper. You've used me just like they have."

"I tried to protect you from all this, tried to let you go like you wanted."

She ignored the way Grendel's broken voice gutted her. "How long will this take?"

Odym's hand tightened over hers with surprising strength, and a warm smile lifted his solemn face. "To defeat the monster, you must embrace the monster within."

The sound of chains and howling beasts trapped in their cells drew their attention. Vynasha placed a hand on Odym's shoulder. "Go before you're discovered. I'll be fine if I am what you say."

"Remember, you came to us with power already inside of you," Odym said as he retreated to the door. "Never forget."

Vynasha shut the door behind him, watching as Odym fiddled with the latch and set the door bar back in place. She could hear the chains as he linked them together again. She clung to the bars covering the small window at the top half of the door, and after a moment, Odym clasped her fingers.

"I shall come to you again when I can," he said.

Vynasha gave him her best smile. "I'll do my best not to fade."

Odym gasped at the sound of a loud crash and howl some distance away. "I must go. They will pick up my scent, and with the gatekeeper injured, I must warn the others."

She peered after the glow his form gave off in the darkness.

CHAPTER TWENTY

A Wylder Tale

"VYNASHA? ARE YOU awake?" Grendel whispered to her through the hole in their wall.

Vynasha lay against the opposite end of her cell, curled in a pile of stale furs. She clutched what remained of Odym's offering to her chest and flinched at the sound of his voice. "Liar," she whispered and watched the play of violet light dance through thin veins. Odym claimed she was already changing, but how long until she transformed?

And what will I become?

"I never wanted to burden you like this," Grendel confessed with a sigh. "After you came, I tried to stay away from you for as long as I could. And after… I hoped our bond might save you from this fate."

She lifted her head and sat up further, ignoring the faint tremble in her limbs. "You weren't going to tell me, were you? You would sacrifice everyone's lives when you could have simply explained what I had to do to save us all!"

"I have tried before!" Their shared wall trembled as he panted, and power flickered between their bond. She felt his rage and heard his despair as he continued, "I have tried so many times, Vynasha, and every time have failed. Tell me, what purpose would there be, asking you to sacrifice yourself? You, who are so full of broken promises, deserve to live most of all. Eventually, we will fade or turn as we were meant to, like Soraya, like all the others who came before you."

Rage unlike anything she had known pushed her limbs to close the distance as she crawled over to their shared hole. "You are so *bleeding* selfish! Don't you care at all about the people here? Because they are people, gatekeeper, no matter their skins. Yes, even Ferox. They live and breathe just like us. To say I'm an exception, that their lives don't count…" She shivered again as anger rippled through her and squeezed her eyes shut.

"How can you continue defending that beast?" Grendel snapped.

"He's not the monster *you* are," she snarled. "He didn't create a blood bond with me against my will." She savored the heavy silence and Grendel's shuddered breath. She hoped he choked on his guilt.

"This is the curse talking through you," he finally said. "Do not let it control you."

She choked on a laugh. "No, Odym said I must embrace it. Our bond might have kept the curse at bay, but I'm not going to fight it anymore."

"Why give in when I am offering you a way out of this hell?"

She clenched her teeth to hold back the tremble in her voice. "Magick is in our blood, Grendel. You don't get to undo your history or forsake your family, and neither will I."

He was silent, and part of her cheered to have stumped him. But that was when the voices trapped within the castle returned.

"*If you embrace this, there is no going back.*"

"I know," she replied.

"Who are you talking to?" Grendel said.

"You smell like fear," she muttered then groaned as her muscles seized. A searing, white-hot pain shot through her head, and she could no longer hear the gatekeeper crying her name. Bursts of fragmented light filled her vision until darkness took over.

Ceddrych's tall shoulders blocked the sunlight, and she giggled as she followed him down the slope toward their cave.

"Wait, Ceddrych! Wait for me!"

He laughed, the sun glinting off his shoulder-length brown hair. It shone like the tarnished gold coins Old Ced kept in his pocket. Sometimes, he took the coins out to count them before bed. Since Mother had passed, his counting often dragged into the night. But Vynasha didn't like to dwell too much on her father or his plans. She pumped her short legs harder to catch up with Ceddrych's longer stride.

"Slow down! You're too fast!"

But Ceddrych did not stop or turn around. He ducked suddenly behind a copse of fir trees.

Vynasha opened her mouth to cry for him again when she tripped on a root and fell face first into the autumn leaves. She groaned as she pushed off the earth and froze at the heaving snarl that sounded ahead of her. She glanced through her tangled hair, unwilling to call for Ceddrych lest the beast be nearby. She dug her fingers into the earth and bit down too hard on her tongue as labored steps accompanied the great beast's approach. Its shadow filled the space between the trees. Tears leaked from her eyes and stained her filthy cheeks.

"Please," she whispered.

The creature paused, and she squeezed her eyes shut as it approached. Its breath was hot against her neck. She shivered as her limbs began to spasm. When no attack came, she opened her eyes to face the earth, and claws grew from her fingertips.

She let loose a scream for her brother, but the only sound that escaped her throat was a bellowing roar. Panicked, she tore the earth to escape, to find him and a way out of this nightmare.

Bitter roars tore Vynasha from the fever dream. She tried to open her eyes, but her limbs continued to spasm. The metallic tang of blood wetted her lips. The roars blurred, and as she struggled past the fever, she could almost hear voices in their snarls.

"Please, help us…free us."

The voices sounded familiar, like the whispering tapestries, like the walls.

"Free us, Beauty. You are the only one who can."

She had been listening to them since her arrival, beckoning her. No longer the faded spirits but rather trapped spirits in cruelly wrought flesh.

"The curse will swallow us whole and tear this decayed city to the ground."

"…our last hope."

"Vynasha!" Grendel's pained cry was hoarse from shouting.

"Grendel," she whimpered. Her bones broke with a resounding snap, and her vision blotted as her consciousness floated beyond the agony.

Ceddrych ran ahead of her, so close she could almost see the shape of the furs he wore. He ran through the Wylder Mountains, chasing something beyond his grasp.

"Ceddrych, wait for me!" she called, but the sound came out as a low growl only she could comprehend.

He turned to face her, still, eyes wide and flashing from brown to luminous green. She flinched from the fear in his eyes as he pulled out a long, thick blade from his side and held the point out between them.

"Stay back!" he warned.

She tried to speak his name, only to hear the beast instead. Black-tipped claws rose to graze her lip instead of hands, eliciting a scream which became a roar too terrible to bear.

"Vynasha!" Grendel shouted, again pulling her from the bizarre visions that plagued her.

She shivered and held her arms to her chest. Her bones were raw and undone, as though she had been broken and knit back together again. Grendel's cries brought her back from the brink of another pain-induced blackout. This time, she clung to the sound of his voice as he called another name.

"Soraya! You have no right to steal what is mine. My blood protects her. I swear by every power I possess you shall not take her from me!"

And the walls whispered back, "*She was never yours to possess.*"

A dozen other voices joined together, beckoning. "*Remember who you are.*"

"Grendel?" she gasped as her muscles tightened and released again.

"I will not let her do this to you!" Grendel bellowed, and a thud followed his cry with the shifting of rocks. "I swear, I shall tear the foundations of this bloody castle apart if she tries to take you!"

"No," she groaned and rolled onto her back. Her bones shifted again, snapping to pieces throughout her body. "Just let me go."

"Never," Grendel growled, and she could almost taste his urge to change. He was trying to harness it, to use the beast's strength to break the wall between them.

Only then did Vynasha realize how greatly the enchantments of the castle had weakened. Soraya's curse contained them all to a degree, but Grendel had power of his own. She knew this because his power flowed in her veins, along with the agony he shared with her.

The other beasts snarled and howled with increasing fervor. Now, she heard the words hidden in souls trapped by enchanted flesh. Some cursed her name, but others begged her for freedom.

Her human nails broke, and stronger black nails grew in their place, sharpening as she dug into stone. Tears of blood spilled from her eyes as she fought the blackness with every fiber of her being.

"Do not give in, Vynasha," Grendel snarled and pounded against the rocks separating them.

The floor trembled, and she cried out.

"*Remember*," the other beasts called through growls and snarls.

"Remember," she gasped.

Wynyth's words echoed in her fractured mind. "*To give life requires sacrifice, little starling.*"

"Please don't leave me." Grendel sobbed against the wall. His pain was hers in that cusp between life and death. His blood in her veins whispered to her of all he kept hidden, the secret he had coveted above all.

"I beg of you," Grendel pleaded, his voice more beast than man.

This is why you bound and chained up the others.

She thought of the other trapped beasts, who had been prisoners as she had. The magick in their blood had not been strong enough to keep them from turning or fading, too diluted over the lifespan of an ancient curse.

This is why I will free them.

"Fight it, Vynasha!"

"No," she growled as the tension in her body slipped away.

The shift was painless in the end, welcome even, like slipping on a comfortable skin.

With every breath her reformed lungs took in, Vynasha's body adjusted to the changes the curse had wrought. New muscles corded and lengthened her limbs. Flat teeth sharpened against her tongue, and each lungful of air overloaded her senses with unfamiliar scents and sensations.

Vynasha opened her new eyes to find the blackness of her cell did not appear as inky but marked by different shapes and shades. She stumbled to her feet and held up her hands, relieved by how normal they appeared, save for sharp black claws.

Like Ferox, she thought with a pang.

Her soiled dress clung to her altered form. The exposed skin of her arms and hands was without fur yet still scarred as before.

She took uneasy steps toward the wall she shared with Grendel, unused to the supple strength of this body, and crouched to find him caught within the change.

Grendel shook as his skin split and fur sprouted then faded in patches as he growled deeply. The truth he had kept from her, that which she sensed through their bond, played out in awful clarity before her.

"Grendel." Her voice came out as a deeper rasp, but it was still hers.

The gatekeeper gasped as he twisted to see her through the gap in stone, the unnatural glow in his eyes and sharpened teeth betraying the change. "Vynasha? How are you still…"

"Are you truly surprised? We're bound by blood now." Her claws pricked her palms as she bared her teeth. "You should have trusted me from the beginning."

More rocks broke free of the wall as he sank against his chains and closed his eyes. "I could not watch it happen again. Please believe I only have tried to protect you."

"If that's true, then tell me the truth. You were the beast that chased me to the castle, weren't you? You stalked me outside my chambers and kept me from reaching the mirror that night?"

Grendel banged his head against the rock with sudden violence, but she refused to flinch. Instead, she reached through the hole and pressed a clawed hand to his ruined shoulder. He shuddered then sighed into her touch. "I am not the only beast that has haunted your steps, but I was the first *she* made."

As though his words had summoned them, the other voices pressed to the back of Vynasha's mind behind their ongoing roars. She pulled her hand free with a snarl. "You kept them chained up like rabid dogs to be put down."

Grendel choked on broken laughter. "Now you see why I arrived bloodied to your chamber, Ash."

"Don't call me that," she hissed, rage ripping hot and vicious through their bond. "You stole that name as you stole my brother's letters."

"And has my blood not been payment enough, Vynasha?"

She gripped her soiled golden skirts. "Did you offer your other victims the same?"

"They were not my victims," he growled back. "I have not had a choice since my mother cursed us and my sworn knight betrayed me."

Vynasha's claws tore her skirts as she stumbled to her feet. "Your mother… no, you're lying! Ferox is the prince."

"Is that what he told you?" Grendel's profile twisted, and his eyes flashed golden. "That old wolf is naught but my mother's *servant*. He only rules now because I gave up my power."

"I don't believe you," she snapped.

Grendel laughed again. "Believe what you wish, Ash. I would have spared you from this curse if you had only run when you had the chance. Now, you are doomed with the rest of us."

"If we are doomed, it's because of you, Grendel. Soraya may have created this curse, but the great evil Wolfsbane warned me about was made by *you*."

New ears picked up the hitch in Grendel's breath as he struggled for words. And Vynasha couldn't say why her conviction hurt as badly as Ferox's betrayal.

She backed away until her back pressed against her cell door. Distant torchlight illuminated the hall beyond. And still, there was that other, sixth sense that allowed her to hear the words hidden in the beasts' cries, pulling at her, pleading with her.

"*Please help us…*"

"*… so dark and lonely.*"

"I should have kept my birthright and stopped this from happening," Grendel finally said. "I am so sorry I failed you."

She turned toward his voice, to his light pouring through the hole he had made what seemed a lifetime ago. "You didn't fail me," she whispered. "I don't think you could have stopped my coming here. And none of you *called* me. I came because of my brother."

"And do you not hate me?"

"I want to," she confessed, but she couldn't bring herself to say her bond with Grendel had protected her. Bitter as the realization was, cruel and wicked as she knew Grendel to be, she couldn't deny their bond changed things. Had Grendel ever tried to bond his blood with another of his beasts? Or had they all turned monstrous because of his attempts?

"Your imprisonment and transformation are the result of my arrogance," came his hoarse reply.

"Arrogance…" Vynasha laughed and turned toward the bars of her prison. "You are only arrogant enough to believe I'm here because of you."

Grendel hesitated, and she could smell his fear. "What do you mean?"

Vynasha wrapped her clawed fingers around the bars and smiled at the newfound strength in her grip. "I knew the chance of finding Ceddrych was slim, and my nephew might not survive the journey. But I came because your people are right about one thing. My mother's blood flows through me. She taught me enough to know great magick requires great sacrifice. And your sacrifice has given me the strength to become what I needed."

"Needed for what?" Grendel snapped.

"Now that I have the power Odym promised, nothing can stop me from freeing them and finding my brother. Not you and certainly not Ferox."

"Wait, Vynasha, please! There is still so much you do not

understand. I have not had a chance to explain, but you must *not* break the wards of this prison!"

A monstrous snarl ripped past her throat as she took several steps back from the door. "If you didn't want me to break the wards, you never should have given me a part of your power, gatekeeper."

She braced her bare feet on the stone floor and then, with all the strength she could muster, ran her body against the barred door. Wood splintered, cracked, and quickly gave under her brute force.

Laughter escaping her lips rippled and swelled into a triumphant howl which drowned out Grendel's protests. The other beasts joined her in their eagerness. She knew the lust for blood for the first time and then understood the temptation to give in to the animal.

"I'll free you all," she growled as her heart pounded fresh blood through new, enhanced limbs.

"No, you condemn us all!" Grendel called after her, but it was too late.

CHAPTER TWENTY-ONE

A Beastly Beauty

SHE LEAPT PAST the splintered wreckage into the hall and looked up and down. Heavy metal-wrapped wooden doors rattled on their hinges as beasts that had slept for half an age woke.

"Yes! Free us!"

Vynasha ran to the end of the hall. Using the power burning through her veins along with her clawed fists, she tore each magick-protected door down until her hands were stained with her blood. Luminous trails stained fallen doors and dripped to the floor, but the creatures she freed did not attack her.

Beasts of every size and shape. Some resembled bears or wolves or great cats, but most seemed a blend, falling somewhere between. And still others with fur in shades of blue-black or smoky purple looked unlike any creature she'd read or heard of.

"Come! You're free!" she urged them.

A few of the beasts inside clung to dark corners, their glowing eyes weak and frightened. Others eagerly helped her break their bonds.

She discovered her claws were preternaturally sharp and best for slicing rusted chains. Soraya's antiquated curse couldn't hold against her power. Every time she defied the curse by freeing them, Vynasha grew stronger.

"Follow me!" she growled as she freed the last, the one in the cell opposite hers. The door was heavier than most, the chains newer than the others. A black, red-eyed beast watched her with almost malevolent satisfaction but did not shift from its place in the opposite corner of the cell. She pushed aside his almost-familiar scent as she finally turned to Grendel's cell without waiting to watch this one flee with the others.

Through the bars, his luminous eyes found hers, golden and shaped like the beast of his other form. His smile revealed faintly sharp teeth. "Have you come to free me too, Vynasha? Or to kill me?"

"I haven't decided." Vynasha hissed as she reached for the chains on his door, only to press against an invisible barrier.

A whimper escaped her throat as she pulled back her fists and tried again. Yet her hands met that invisible force, vibrating as she struggled to break through the magick barring her way. She cursed her frustration then stilled when Grendel slowly rose to his feet. The long chains keeping him bound to the wall rattled as he came to the center of the cell until his arms pulled taut. One chain had already torn a chunk from the wall they had shared and lay useless on the dungeon floor.

Grendel's face was marked by half-healed claw marks and swollen welts, but his weary voice betrayed the depths of his condition. He turned a pale, illuminated hand to reveal the recent slash crossing his palm, a ragged cut over dozens of healed scars. "Forgive me, Vynasha, but I cannot let you in."

"You forget we are bound. I will break your ward in time," she said, her words barely distinguished above the growls spilling from her throat.

His beastly eyes glistened. "You spoke true when you said great magick requires great sacrifice. And once you leave me, I will quickly lose control over myself. So I cannot allow you to free me, Vynasha. You *must* flee this place before the curse takes possession of all of you. I only pray you might forgive me for all the pain my selfishness has brought you." His eyes roamed over her features as though to memorize her. "All of you."

Vynasha hissed and tried to bring a clawed fist against the door, only to beat at the air again. She couldn't be certain what choice she might have made had she broken into his cell. By giving in to her instincts, she had lost part of her reasoning. But this did not affect her understanding.

Grendel shut his eyes, and tears spilled over his cheeks. "Leave me, Vynasha. Leave us to ruin and do not come back."

Wynyth once told her that words held powerful magic. True names once given could be used to claim and control in the wrong hands. Grendel's command spilled past his lips and resonated with their shared blood, tugged at her limbs, and forced them to comply.

Vynasha cried out as their bond, once made to heal, compelled her body to turn away from his cell. And like a fool, she had given enough of herself to Grendel that she could not fight him in her current state.

As her legs carried her away, she glimpsed the other beasts rushing toward the stairs leading to the upper levels of the castle. Their need to break and rend spoke to her own need for vengeance, but Grendel's command forced her in the opposite direction.

Vynasha bit her tongue as her body betrayed her again. Beneath the heady power and beastly urges, a small voice within wondered.

What will they do to Dragos?

To Hvalla and Odym and the other wylderfolk?

What will they do to Ferox?

Vynasha refused to regret breaking his victims' chains, but a small part of her festered in fear. Grendel was too broken to stop the force of bloodlust in their hearts, and now, he had sent her away.

Tears stole her vision as she was forced to run past the prison and down another path. None of this was familiar to her but belonged to the gatekeeper's memory hidden deep in her veins. Her new legs and Grendel's compulsion made her run faster, taking twists and turns she eventually gave up fighting.

A chorus of mighty roars trickled down from the castle high above, jarring her sensitive ears. It was the sound of a battle she was denied and a reminder. No matter how strong she might become, magick or no, Grendel's command reminded her of the truth behind who he was.

The selfish prince, damned by his own mother.

The great evil that drew innocents into his lair like a demon.

The gatekeeper who had thrust his power upon a hated servant.

Now she, too, had to obey him. Was this why he'd allowed the bond where he refused others?

The thought struck a nerve in more than one disturbing way. Much as Ferox had tried to orchestrate his courtship with her, Grendel manipulated her in a different manner.

And you started to believe you cared for him, stupid, naïve girl.

The farther she ran, the more her bond with the gatekeeper dimmed.

She cursed him for giving her this bond which allowed her to hold on to herself rather than give in to mindless, beastly instinct.

She cursed him for choosing for her.

Only when she entered a level below the dungeons, into a cavern crusted with precious gems and echoing the rush of the underground river, did her steps slow. And only once the compulsion lifted did she realize she had not traveled alone.

Hot breath grazed the back of her neck. Vynasha slowly turned to meet a pair of knowing ruby eyes, surrounded by razorback-black fur, a terrifying cross between a bear and something not of this earth. It was the last beast she had freed before attempting to release Grendel.

He alone had ignored the others in their need for revenge, choosing to follow her instead. Whatever bond allowed her to comprehend these creatures was eerily silent now. As she drew in another breath and a familiar scent awash with the dungeons and snows of the forest, Vynasha recalled her mad flight to the castle.

Something had stalked her through the forest then, something that forced her and Dragos to the castle.

Still, the creature made no move to harm her. Drawing in a steadying breath, Vynasha said, "Are you here to finish me off, then?"

The black beast followed with a lumbering, eerily silent gait. Knowing red eyes held her and spoke of boundless hatred and something which stirred deeper beneath the surface.

"If you're not going to kill me, I suppose you could come with me."

The black beast cocked its head as though listening, and then the voice came as a deep rumble from its throat and to her mind. "*I will follow.*"

Vynasha's breath caught, and her fists tightened over her ruined skirts. "What is your name?"

A shallow rumble vibrated in its gullet, and the voice reached her again. "*I am called Grolthox.*"

Vynasha couldn't hide her shudder at the name she barely recalled from passing moments and conversations not intended for her ears. She pushed all lingering fear she felt into the same dark space in which she kept memories of the fire that stole her family.

Keeping her lips pressed closed over a tentative smile, she came to step alongside Grolthox.

"I am Vynasha," she said. "I'm glad you have decided not to eat me."

"*Perhaps I will later,*" the beast replied, but his malice seemed to fade with the threat.

Still, a part of Vynasha breathed easier when Grolthox gave no sign of attack, keeping pace with her. "I'm not sure why you'd choose to follow me," she added with a low whisper. "I don't know where this path leads, and I'm not sure where to begin looking for my family."

Grolthox remained silent at first, and so she started when the beast's reply came. "*Family will find you.*"

Vynasha swallowed past the ache in her throat. "And will they even recognize me?" She shook her head as she tried to imagine Wyll's reaction. If Wolfsbane allowed her to get close…

Grolthox nudged her clawed hand with his wet maw. "*I am here.*"

She flinched then reached a trembling hand to lie over the beast's neck. "I would find that more reassuring if you weren't planning to eat me."

"*Not today,*" Grolthox replied.

Vynasha smiled as the beast leaned into her touch and focused on the path ahead.

In these kinds of caves, one wrong turn could lead her into a pit, a blind beast's den, or walls so narrow they threatened to crush her chest. This was nothing like the cave she and Ceddrych had discovered and spent hours in, away from their meddlesome family. That cave had led into the smaller peaks that surrounded Whistleande, but they knew better than to explore too deeply. Ceddrych once said that there were places underneath the earth where the air was poisonous to breathe. He told her that he knew because Wynyth had once found him in such a place when he was a small boy.

"They searched for me all over the valley, Ash, even Old Ced. But Mother was the one to find me. She never told me how she knew I was asleep at the back of that cave. But when I woke up, she told me what happened. And she warned me never to venture into blackness alone."

So, naturally, he had dragged Vynasha with him as soon as she could wander the hills. They had explored for hours, noting which hidden rooms were covered by ancient markings and crude tools and old bones. Though he was older than she was by nigh on a decade, Ceddrych seemed to find childlike joy in sharing his old haunts with her. She claimed it was only because he needed someone to share in his strangeness.

She could almost hear him now, saying, *"You know me well, little sister."*

Now, she was venturing into the blackness with eyes that could see in the dark and a monster at her side, just like one of her brother's old tales. And in light of all she had learned, she wondered if there had been more to Wynyth's warning than Ceddrych understood.

"What if we were always more than mortal man?"

She didn't know she'd spoken aloud until Grolthox chuffed. *"Danger ahead."*

Vynasha flexed her fist to avoid jumping out of her skin. She had gained power far beyond anything Wynyth could have imagined for her, and still, she struggled to remain vigilant of her surroundings.

Those red eyes blinked slowly as Vynasha realized the beast was practically leaning against her, as the path had turned too narrow for them to walk alongside one another.

"You're right, it's too small," she said with a grimace. She scraped a clawed hand against the gem-encrusted wall. "Maybe you should go first?" she asked.

Grolthox tossed his head and nudged her forward, nose to the small of her back.

Vynasha rolled her eyes but obeyed. "Only if you promise not to bite me."

"*Fear the one that hunts us more.*"

"But you were the only one who followed me," she said.

"*He will not be able to let you go,*" Grolthox replied with a huff.

Vynasha pressed a hand against the cavern wall and ignored the sudden stench of her fear. "Let's worry about that once we find a way out of this labyrinth." Not when she needed to focus on the path ahead and the unpredictable beast at her side.

The cave became almost too narrow in many places but widened the deeper they traveled. A low, ever-present flow of water echoed off the walls. "Maybe this was part of an underground river passage?" she mused aloud. "A way for the family to escape from attack above."

"*Faster,*" Grolthox snorted and pushed her forward until she stumbled.

"If you wanted to move more quickly, you should have gone first," she called over her shoulder. She didn't enjoy keeping her back to the beast, not when he was the same one that had pursued her so doggedly on her journey. "Maybe someday, you'll tell me why you were so determined I reach the castle."

She still hadn't decided whether she wanted to curse Grolthox for driving her to her fate or to thank him. If anything, it had been the bloody beggar in Whistleande that started all of this. Him and the voice in the wind. Her heart stuttered at the thought of Ferox, of the lack of noise from above reaching them here, in the belly of the world. She thought of the kindness he'd shown and the violence with which he later forced her to claim the mirror. Vynasha's claws scraped against the walls, and she closed her eyes to banish the memory.

It was then she heard it for the first time—the pounding of water falling on rocks.

"Do you hear that?" she whispered.

Grolthox purred low and pressed his nose to her back again. "*Close to the border.*"

Vynasha darted forward until the sound grew from a pounding to a roar. Before she could see it clearly, the spray of the waterfall hit her face, briefly clearing her vision. Though the cave was still dark, she could see the ceiling curve over like cooling metal into the water. The floor draped just shy of the edge, and they kept close to the opposite wall of the little room.

Relief filled her as quickly as the fresh air in her lungs. Laughter bubbled up in her throat and tore from her lips in a sob as she collapsed in a heap against the cave floor. Water droplets misted over her skin, reminding her they had made it.

"I'll find you soon, Wyll," she whispered. "I swear it."

Grolthox prowled past her to inspect the edges of their temporary haven. "*Cannot stay long,*" he warned.

"I know. Just give me a moment." Vynasha rubbed the moisture from her face with the edge of her torn skirt and laughed again. "I can't believe we found a way out."

The beast grunted low in agreement as he returned to her side, keeping his face toward the way they had come. "*Others will follow.*"

Vynasha nodded and brought her hand to the beast's flank again. "What about the wylderfolk, the other servants? Do you think they'll be okay?"

A flare of bitter fury flickered in the mental connection between them, and Grolthox remained silent.

Vynasha leaned her head against the wall and stared at the precious gems glittering like stars around them. "I understand why you hate them, but they're still people like us."

"*We are monsters,*" Grolthox argued with a warning growl.

She ran a soothing hand over his raised hackles. "Maybe we are, but even monsters deserve to be free."

No sooner had she spoken than something pulsed painfully against the skin of her chest. She cried out in pain and tore at her neck until she pulled the chain free. The amulet flashed so brightly violet light filled the room, temporarily blinding them.

Grolthox's lips peeled back over rows of savage teeth, and a snarl broke the pounding of the nearby falls. "*I warned you.*"

She couldn't pull the amulet over her head. The chain remained bound to her, and the stone pulsed an increasing rhythm as the walls around them began to tremble.

Vynasha scrambled back and to her feet as sweat broke out on the back of her neck. "I don't understand! What's happening?"

"*He wants his bride!*" Grolthox roared as dust and rock shook loose as the cavern quaked.

A rock broke free of the glittering ceiling and hit her shoulder. A beastly howl tore from her throat as Vynasha stumbled.

Grolthox shoved her aside before more rock and precious stones fell and shattered onto the ground, shuddering beneath their feet. "*Climb on and do not let go!*"

Vynasha caught fistfuls of fur on his back and clung tightly as black spotted her vision. Somehow, she managed to throw a leg over his flank and braced her weakening limbs around the beast.

Grolthox raced for the crumbling lip of the cavern and into the pounding force of the waterfall.

The beast's roar filled her ears as they tumbled off the edge of the cliff, spilling with the overflow.

Time slowed as water thundered around them, a merciless force pushing them faster. Her heart leapt from her chest as they fell farther still.

Into the river far below, they careened at breaking speed, and she caught a brief glimpse of the shape and form of her death.

Grolthox twisted at the last possible moment, taking the brunt of the impact as they hit the water.

Vynasha didn't dare let go, hooking her claws further into his flesh as the river shoved them down. Water filled her mouth and beat its way down her throat.

The merciless current tossed them against rocks at the riverbed. But Grolthox pushed off the bottom, sending them back up to roll among rapids.

Flashes of trees and mountains were interspaced with the spray of white water before they were shoved under once more and tossed down the current. Only then did the last of Grolthox's considerable strength give out.

When they did not breach again for air, her lungs constricted, threatening to burst.

Her last thought as the blackness took her was for Wyll, who would never know how she lived or died.

JENNIFER SILVERWOOD

Chapter Twenty-Two

A Shattered Heart

DROWNING WAS EASIER than fighting curses. Better to accept death than the constant battle with magick and monsters she had lived with this past moon. Wyll could find safety and maybe even a home with Wolfsbane and his daughter. She could only pray they would care for him better than she. At least now, she would see Wynyth and Tamyra again. Wherever they were could not be as horrible as the world of harsh winters and dark curses she was leaving behind.

Do witches go to heaven?

She waited for the saints to take her, to see the faces of her family she had slowly forgotten.

A dull ache throbbed in her back and at her neck instead. Tingling sensations pricked at her limbs until she turned to face the earth. Water trapped in her lungs was exorcised until her throat burned and her sore lungs dragged in fresh, cool air.

Vynasha blinked against the bright light of day and pushed with quivering limbs against the mud, only to sink onto her elbows. Faced with her clawed and bloody fingertips, realization flooded her and spilled tears down her cheeks, as though the river was still escaping her body however it could. She spat the last of it and laid her cheek against the frozen mud as she waited for her heartbeat to calm.

How am I still alive?

As her vision cleared, the dark blur beside her slowly sharpened. She stiffened and tried to push off the mud and ice.

"Grolthox?" But the longer she stared, the less beastly the creature appeared, until there was only a naked man lying in a pool of black fur and blacker blood. His wrinkled skin was marred by violent scars and bruises, so his face was almost unrecognizable from his wounds. Yet something about him, much like his scent, was terribly familiar.

"No," she said in a broken rasp even as she crawled to his side over sharp rocks.

The man turned his head, and his bright-blue eyes widened as he reached for her with a bloody hand. "Vynasha."

"Father," she said as she took his hand in hers.

"Wynyth's girl…" Old Ced took in her altered appearance with mortal eyes. "Forgive me for failing you."

"Don't," she hissed as she thought of the fire. "You don't need *my* forgiveness."

"I ask all the same and beg you let me explain, little starling."

"You never came back." Tears burned behind her eyes, but she would not give in to them this time. "You took Ceddrych, and you *left us behind.* You should have been there!"

Her father's gaze grew heavy as he struggled to speak. Blood streaked out his nose and past his lips. "I couldn't escape this cursed land… not unless I gave them something in return."

Vynasha's throat ached as though the river yet filled it. "So your greed trapped you, but what happened to Ceddrych?"

"Told him to stay behind. Boy never crossed through the castle gates. Expected a ruin, and the prince found me instead. So I made a bargain to spare my life."

Ice filled her veins. She dug her claws into her thighs just shy of piercing skin, just enough to make certain this wasn't another nightmare. "Me," she spat out between clenched teeth. "You gave him me."

"Saints forgive me, I did," her father confessed.

Vynasha resisted the violence battering against her reserve. Had she not broken from imprisonment, been beaten by rocks, and taken a tumble down a waterfall, her beastly side might have won out.

But the sickly scent of his blood and the ache in her soul kept her mind sharp enough. Barely enough to summon compassion for the man her mother had loved.

A strange smile tipped the corner of his mouth. "Wynyth loved you most, so like her in every way… couldn't stand to look at you after she left me."

Vynasha sank further onto the rocks and kept hold of his hand. Even as she realized his blood smelled *wrong* in the way of dark magick and the way of the diseased and dying. And Vynasha at last understood why his abused voice sounded so familiar.

"The beggar in the village. That was you."

"Yes." Old Ced sighed as he clutched her hand. "Prince used the mirror to send me through, long enough to lure you to us. He promised to make you queen."

"You're a bleeding fool," she whispered, unwilling to think of Ferox and how easily she might have become their queen. "All your life, you've craved what you couldn't have, what you thought you were *owed* after Grandfather lost the family fortune."

A wheezing laugh escaped him. "That's what Ceddrych said when he refused to cross the castle gate. Boy never stopped wanting to go home to you." His brief laugh ended in a violent cough that left him struggling for breath.

"Father?" Vynasha helped tilt him to his side.

"Shouldn't have told him the truth about you and Wynyth," he groaned.

"What truth?" Vynasha asked and then cringed when he ran his free hand over her claws.

"Wynyth's blood protected you," he observed, his voice softer, teetering on the edge of his strength. "She ran away from her destiny and paid the price. You weren't my child, but I promised her I could do right by you… Tried to protect you in the castle, too, but I couldn't control my cursed form."

Not his child.

The words were like blades to her heart.

"I promised her… so beautiful," he said with a bloody smile, "most beautiful woman I'd ever seen. She loved my children, and I made a promise before she left me… Wynyth."

Vynasha gathered her father into her lap as best she could. The winds seemed to howl through the forest around them, and the falls roared in the distance, but Vynasha barely noticed. She could not see past her tears and the sudden need to keep him with her.

"Stay." Her voice broke on the word. "Please don't go yet."

"Keep you safe," her father rambled on, his gaze unfocused and unseeing. He squeezed her hand weakly.

Vynasha pressed her lips to his cold cheek. "You kept your promise and came after me in the end. You were going to follow me wherever the path led, remember?"

"I promised Wynyth," he insisted. "I kept my promise…"

"She knows," Vynasha said as his eyes dilated and a final breath escaped his lungs with a shuddering sigh.

Her father died with a smile on his lips, but this did nothing to erase the fact he had broken his promise countless times.

"My father," she whispered, hating that he could still hurt her so deeply after abandoning her time and again. Broken promises were the reason she'd barely considered his fate in coming to Wylderland, too lost in her need to find Ceddrych.

Not my brother.

But if she wasn't Ceddrych's sister and Wyll's aunt, who was she? Where did that leave her?

No one's daughter.

No one's queen.

No one.

Vynasha bit her lip and buried her face in his neck, clinging to her father's lingering warmth. All she had left was the life stealing from his skin and the emptiness of the wylderland around them.

The water flowing nearby spread wide from the embankment and deeper into the forested valley ahead. She wondered if this was the same river she'd been plucked from before. Now she could smell the magick in its waters. Had it somehow stripped her father's enchantment?

Vynasha knew she needed to bury his body and find shelter soon. Only a fool would linger here with winter-starved predators roaming the wood. But each time she summoned the will to set him down, she couldn't.

So she held her father's hand instead until his body turned cold and stiff with the snow falling gently over them.

Would it be so terrible to let it bury us together?

"Mother, I'm so tired…"

The howling wind picked up once more, as if in answer, louder than before.

She shook her head as her vision blurred. "I can't do this anymore, Mother. Please don't make me bury our family again."

All at once, the howling ceased, and the forest fell quiet. Gooseflesh rippled down the back of her neck.

It was never the wind.

The sudden loss of winter sun against her back was almost physical. She turned quickly to see what had cast a shadow.

A deep growl built at the back of her throat, and her arms reflexively tightened around her father's body.

Three wolves, one black and two gray, stood before her, not twenty paces off the embankment. Their hackles raised, they remained motionless, assessing with eyes which glowed an unnatural green.

Like Ferox.

Vynasha bared her teeth, and the amulet about her neck dimly glowed. If the beasts had hoped for easy prey, they were mistaken. Exhaustion had settled into her limbs, true, but she had strength enough for this.

"You can't have him," she snarled as the black-furred wolf slowly approached. "Stay back!"

The gray wolves growled, and the black wolf shuddered as it came to a halt far too close. Near enough to lunge and bite. Yet the beast made no move to attack, only sniffed at her father, and met her gaze with intelligent eyes.

Whatever power connected her to Grendel's beasts did not hold sway with these wolves. She heard no words hidden behind their yips and growls. Still, something in the black wolf's eyes compelled her to try.

"Please," she whispered to the great wolf. "Let me bury him, then you can have me."

Any strength she imagined within herself must have been far less than she commanded. That or the rocks that battered her in the cave finally took effect. Or so she believed as the wolf before her suddenly changed form from beast to man.

Unlike her own painful transformation, the wolf's black fur

simply loosened and spread into a heavily lined cloak that hung over the man's broad shoulders. Past shaggy hair and a full beard, familiar golden-green eyes found hers, and all breath stole from her lungs.

Ceddrych.

She blinked against the vision before her, afraid to speak and shatter this delusion. Yet her lips formed his name around a growing smile.

Thank you, Mother.

Even if this were her mind playing tricks, if this be the face death chose to greet her with, she would welcome him with open arms.

The changeling—for that was what he must surely be—approached her with careful steps. He looked quite different from the brother she remembered. His face was riddled with new lines, and hardened eyes practically screamed his disbelief.

Yet as the changeling looked from her father to Vynasha's shivering form, his gaze softened. He reached for her with trembling hands. A familiar honeyed voice, rough as though from disuse, filled the space between them. "You can let him go, now, Ash. We'll bury him, and then he can rest."

"Ceddrych," she sobbed as she released their father and leaped into his arms.

She clung as tightly as her fading strength allowed, mindless of her claws or the disgust he must surely feel. But his arms caught her easily and held her as though she weighed nothing. He wasn't pushing her away.

What would Ceddrych say when she told him of all that happened, what she'd become, what their father had said? The words were on the tip of her tongue, but the furs and Ceddrych's warm body were too comforting.

"I'm never letting you go again, Ash," he promised.

Together.

She shut her eyes and welcomed oblivion.

CHAPTER TWENTY-THREE

A Bittersweet End

BEASTS HAUNTED HER dreams, snarling and clawing after her flesh and wearing her father's broken face. She ran from him, begging forgiveness, begging that she might finally forgive him. Sometimes, Wynyth's magick came to life in her limbs, making her skin glow in violet shades until she remembered she was a beast too. Her cries became Grolthox's haunting snarls, and something flickered at the edge of her conscience, something important she needed to remember.

"*Remember,*" the voices had said.

Wyll floated in and out of her nightmares, giving her hope when her soul couldn't bear the sorrow any longer.

"*I dreamed I fought a wolf, Asha,*" he once told her.

"*Who won?*"

"*I did, but the wolf killed me too…*"

"I'd kill any wolf that came near you and skin it myself," she'd promised.

"Wyll," she whispered.

A warm, familiar voice spoke through her delusions. "Rest, Asha. You're safe now." It sounded like Ceddrych, and therefore it must be yet another illusion she was happy to give in to.

Time slipped past like water through her fingers, like the magick forcing her spirit to meld with her cursed form. Vynasha couldn't tell how long she drifted in that in-between place of dreams and memories. Strange voices spoke in low murmurs over her in the dark, but her eyes barely opened to blurred, luminous figures.

Whispers in the dark had haunted her ever since she came to the castle, so the voices didn't frighten her. And so it wasn't the voices or even the howling snarls that disturbed her rest but the thick, suffocating silence.

She came back into her new body slowly. Her fingers sought purchase on the hilt of the dagger Ferox had gifted her but found fur blankets instead. Her claws slashed at the covers as she jerked fully awake with a gasp.

The fire burning at the center of the one-room cottage exposed little of her smoky surroundings. The cot she lay in sat against a log wall on one end with a short bookshelf lining one side. Meat and herbs swung gently from the rafters. Smoke rose through a small hole above, but the air was still permeated by a foul stench. Her new senses made her eyes water and the bitter taste of ash coat her tongue.

Vynasha shuddered as the scent summoned memories of scalding ash and the scent of burning flesh. Determined to build space between herself and the fire, she threw back her covers and stood on unsteady legs. Where was the animal strength that had given her the means to escape the castle? She grasped the cabin wall and followed the rough texture until she found a groove, a crack that framed the closed doorway. Desperation for clean air pushed her to force the door open.

She threw up her hands against the blinding sunlight as she stumbled into the unknown. Her snugly wrapped feet sank into ankle-deep snow, and her arms flailed as she sought her bearings.

Voices called out in the near distance, and she hesitated. Hopefully, her sight would adjust to the sunlight soon so she could judge what sort of people they were. The villagers had not often been kind in Whistleande.

The outline of trees took the shape of gray silhouettes, and figures darted to and from cottages separated by a path between. At her approach, they froze.

Vynasha gasped as her vision cleared to reveal the wylderfolk. Some had hooves instead of booted feet and fawn-like spots along their sides, while others looked normal but for feathers growing from their heads instead of hair. They were beautiful and strange, but the ones who looked most mortal appeared out of place beside these people of fable. It was as though the whispering tapestries in the castle had come to life.

An old man with ebony skin scratched one of two horns sprouting from his forehead.

Horns like Ferox wore.

A small boy with green skin screamed, and his mother scooped him up in her arms, the vines twisting her raven hair and glinting gold in the sunlight.

Vynasha stumbled and braced her fall with trembling hands as hot tears burned in her eyes.

Witch, they had whispered behind her back in her home village of Whistleande. While all had loved her roses, they'd kept their children a safe distance from her, the cursed witch who grew everlasting roses.

Even among these people, I'm a monster.

She sank to her knees and grabbed a fist full of snow.

"Look at her hands, Mummy!" a child cried.

"Keep away, Klevas," hissed a woman. "She is one of the cursed."

"Ash?" A deep, warm voice pulled her from the memory of children screaming.

Vynasha shuddered as Ceddrych cupped her face with calloused hands and brushed her tears away.

She covered his hand with hers in wonder and grief as she whispered his name.

Ceddrych shook his head, and his brow furrowed with concern. "Ash, what are you doing out of bed? You're going to freeze if we don't get you beside a fire." He lifted her in his arms as though she weighed nothing.

"Where are we?" She stared at her new hand resting over his heart and ignored the rumbling whispers of the gathering crowd. "Where is Father?"

"Buried as he should have been moons ago," he managed between clenched teeth. "And this is my home." He favored the villagers with a harsh glare as he carried her toward the cottage door she'd fled.

"Don't take me back there." She buried her head in his fur cloak and breathed in the scent of him. "Too much smoke."

"Of course… I should have known." Sorrow coated his words, and something dark flashed through his hazel eyes as they traced her scars.

She ran her fingertips over his beard and felt his sharp exhale. "This is real?"

Rather than be disgusted by her claws, Ceddrych's expression softened, and he held her closer. Close enough she could smell the wolf resting beneath his human skin, could scrutinize the fine detail of a face once called boyishly handsome and now lined by a harsh life. A scar on his left cheek also dented the bridge of his nose. His brown hair had grown long enough for him to tie part of it behind his neck, and his skin was a darker russet than she remembered.

"Am I much changed, Ash?" he asked, gaze flickering between her eyes and her smile.

Vynasha shook her head. "Not to me."

"Wanderer!"

Ceddrych tensed and hissed through his teeth, "Keep your eyes down, no matter what he says to provoke us."

Another changeling came to stand before them, smelling strongly of both wolf and human. Vynasha closed her eyes and breathed in deeply to take in the stranger's scent. Silver firs and raging rivers met her nose, along with undercurrents of fury and subtle fear.

"I allowed you to bring this cursed child into our midst," the man snarled, "so long as you keep her contained. We cannot risk her unleashing her dark magick on the village nor bring our enemies upon us."

"I never needed your permission to bring my *sister* home, Balos," Ceddrych growled. "And I was already bringing her back inside, as you can see."

Balos leaned closer and sniffed. "Tread carefully, Wanderer. The elders may favor you, but never forget *I* control the pack."

"Perhaps you should go deal with your pack, then, and leave us to our own affairs." Ceddrych turned his back on the changeling and stalked back to his cottage.

"She will never be welcomed here, Wanderer," Balos called after them. "The cursed can never be one of us!"

A terrible shudder passed through her brother's limbs, only calming when Ceddrych pressed his nose to her forehead and breathed in deeply.

Vynasha turned to peek over his shoulder past the village

homes with their smoking chimney holes and to the jagged horizon. A winter storm brewed tumultuous gray amid the tallest mountain peaks, and for a moment, she could see the outline of the castle.

Leave us to ruin and do not come back.

She curled further into Ceddrych's embrace, relieved once they returned to the cottage.

By leaving the door open, much of the cloying smoke had cleared, though the air was chilled upon their return. The cold rarely bothered her since the fire.

Ceddrych kept hold of her with one arm and closed the latch with the other with surprising force.

"I can walk, you know," she gently teased. Ceddrych had rarely ever been angry before unless Vynasha was being teased by their sisters or mistreated by their father.

Her brother merely grunted as he carried her to the cot she had awakened in.

While she was still wary of the way his limbs shook with repressed fury, Vynasha knew he'd never hurt her. Even now, after they had been so altered by time and magick.

"Are you hungry?" He settled her onto the cot and tucked the furs around her shoulders, his gaze unsettled and darting about the room. "I don't have any of your favorites, but I could ask—"

"Ceddrych, I am quite content." She caught his hand and tugged until he reluctantly sat beside her. "I came all this way for you, not my favorite dishes."

His shoulders heaved as his expression shuttered to her, dark and unfathomable. There was a time when they could read one another's thoughts with a look. A time when she would have climbed into his lap and forced him to tell her what was wrong. She feared what this new distance in his eyes could mean but refused to release him from her hold.

Ceddrych pushed his loose hair back and shook his head. "I

am sorry for what happened out there. I stepped out only a moment to speak with the twins, and then I heard the screams."

"I should have waited." She ducked her head as shame filled her. "I know why I frighten them, Ceddrych. You don't have to apologize."

His rough hand slid along her jaw and tipped her chin until she was forced to look at him. "No, I *do* need to apologize, and not just for today. I need to apologize for being foolish enough to let Father talk me into leaving you."

"Ceddrych." Forgetting her new teeth, she bit her lip. She stuttered when he pulled her lip gently free and caught a bead of violet blood on his thumb.

"Would you tell me what happened?"

Vynasha's breath caught in her chest as they stared at the way her blood gleamed in the firelight. "I don't even know how to begin."

"Tell me," he urged, familiar fondness warming his tone.

She shook her head. "How can you possibly be content with this?"

The lines furrowing his brow deepened. "Content with what?"

"With me," she whispered. "With what I am."

Ceddrych enclosed her hand with both of his and leaned forward. "You are my sister, Vynasha."

She shook her head, tears blurring her gaze. "I am a monster."

His eyes flashed green, revealing a hint of the wolf within the man. "You are my family, and this is my fault."

A laugh bubbled through her at the absurdity of it all. "Forgive me, Ceddrych, but how is what I've become your fault?"

"Terrible as it was to find him with you as he was, I can't say I wasn't also relieved. Father fell ill in the Eirwen Mountains, you see, and *I* allowed him to lead us north. I should have forced him to come home, but I think… I was so angry with him for so long, Vynasha. I don't know if I wanted him to become well in the end."

Painful as it was to hear him speak of their father, with all she had yet to confess, she still asked, "How did you come across the lost city?"

A troubled frown passed over his face. "A hunter came across us while we were setting up camp and warned us to stay far away from the castle." He shook his head. "You can imagine how Old Ced took that. 'No one's been there in ages, and it's ripe for the picking,' he tried to tell me, the bloody fool."

The beggar's broken form haunted her mind, and Vynasha interrupted, "How ill was he?"

Ceddrych traced over her claws. "I believe it was the wasting sickness, but when we came to these mountains and drank from the river, we slowly changed."

Vynasha leaned her head against his shoulder and sighed. "I sensed enchantment in the water."

Ceddrych slipped an arm around her waist and pulled her closer. "I stayed behind with our camp while he went off, searching for stolen silver. Spent maybe a week alone, waiting. I had half a mind to leave the old man and make for home, but I couldn't face the girls without him. Can you imagine what Tamyra would have said?"

At the mention of Tamyra, Vynasha couldn't bear to leave him in ignorance any longer. "Ceddrych…" She waited for his honey-golden eyes to meet hers. The words stuck to her tongue, painful enough to say to strangers, but this was worse. "Our sisters are dead. They—they died in a fire."

Ceddrych's chest rose and fell more rapidly, but he didn't reply, only squeezed her hand, silently bidding her continue.

"I wasn't home when it happened." She closed her eyes to hide her tears. "I was in our cave when the voice woke me." His grip on her waist tightened briefly as she continued, "I smelled smoke first and ran until I could see the flames. I heard screaming and didn't think when I ran inside. Tamyra and Wyll were staying in the attic.

Tamyra was pinned down, but she begged me to take Wyll. I didn't even think of the others, not until much later. The house collapsed after I carried Wyll out."

Wyll hadn't been breathing. The smoke stole him from her before they could escape.

Great magick requires great sacrifice.

"I—I didn't even notice our burns until after," she rasped. "And Wyll's wounds never fully healed." She took a long, shuddering breath and opened her eyes to find Ceddrych's face coated with tears.

He shook his head and caressed the scars on her cheek and trailing down her neck. "I am so bloody sorry, Ash." His voice hitched, and then he pulled her roughly into his arms.

Vynasha clung to him, relieved and hating herself all over again. "Don't! If I hadn't been pouting in our cave like a stupid child, I would have gone to bed last. I would have made sure all the flames were put out. It was my fault. I should have died with them!"

"Never say that!" Ceddrych ran his fingers through her tangled hair. "Maybe you could have stopped the fire from happening, maybe not. You saved Wyll, and you saved *yourself.* That's all that matters now. If you had been in the house, there is no guarantee you wouldn't have died, too, and then I never would have known what happened."

To be held after holding herself together for so long was a bliss Vynasha hadn't expected. Perhaps it would have been easier to continue her self-abhorrence if Ceddrych had raged at her. Instead, he gathered the broken pieces of her and held them in his arms. By sheer stubbornness, he would mend the gaps and smooth the cracks with love.

He whispered to her as her sobs became less fierce. "Maybe none of us is truly at fault for any of this, Ash. We made our choices, and this is what came of them. I gained a pack, and you grew claws and sharp teeth."

Vynasha shook her head. "You *would* try to see the humor

in this." After a pause, she glanced up and smiled. "I'm glad of it. It means you haven't changed too much." His eyes roved her own recent changes, and she shifted uncomfortably beneath his scrutiny.

"My pack was hunting when we picked up your scent by the falls. We never go that close to the castle. The twins never would have followed me if I hadn't pressed on."

"And Balos?"

Ceddrych scoffed. "Our alpha wasn't even in the same territory, off on another hunt."

"Wolves chased me to the castle gates, but I never imagined they were more than wolves."

"You reeked of dark magick. That's why the others won't trust you. I had to fight them before we were allowed back in the village, but I would have done far worse if they denied me." An edge of steel to his voice matched the wildness behind his eyes.

"I thought I would never see you again," she marveled. For the first time, she allowed her mind to entertain thoughts of the fabled Eirwen Mountains and the life they might build there.

Ceddrych's brow rose, and he attempted a weak smile. "I always knew I would find a way back to you, little sister."

Once I find Wyll, we can leave this place, live somewhere better together.

The vision of a homely cottage with Ceddrych and Wyll and roses sprawling over the walls filled her heart. Vynasha's eyes fluttered closed, and she wished as she had never wished so deeply before.

Can I make it real, Mother? Am I strong enough?

Vynasha wanted to tell Ceddrych then, about bringing Wyll and leaving him behind while she went on her foolish quest.

Her smile faded as she felt a hard lump beneath her palm, hidden beneath her shift. As though sensing her awareness, the amulet pulsed beneath her palm. She didn't dare breathe, nor did she pull it free to show her brother.

The villagers had nearly denied her a place because of the curse, because they sensed her bond with Grendel.

"Sleep as long as you need to, Ash. You're safe now," Ceddrych swore with a kiss to her brow.

But Vynasha knew there was no place safe enough, no cave or cottage that would hide her from the prince's wrath.

Will he claim me for his bride as Ferox almost did?

"Sleep," Ceddrych urged as he laid back on the cot with Vynasha in his arms. And as she settled into the comforting furs, her body sank into rest of its own volition, while her heart ached for a love she longed to hate.

Vynasha's journey continues with

SCARRED BEAUTY
(WYLDER TALES: VOL

Preorder your copy today!

Thanks for reading! If you enjoyed *Craving Beauty*, I would be beyond grateful if you could leave an honest review. Long or fortune cookie length, either would be a big help in spreading the word about this series. Thank you for supporting me through this epic journey, fantasy avengers.

Keep reading for a sneak peek of Scarred Beauty…

SCARRED BEAUTY PREVIEW

THE CASTLE HAD always been dark and drafty, but now, the walls rippled and shivered with moonlight. Tiny blue lights drifted ahead of her path, dancing past tapestries that watched her trek through the forbidden halls. Vynasha met their silent gaze and wondered why she heard no sound from the beasts she had set free.

A dimly glowing figure stepped out of the shadows, and she froze, looking down to see if she could pull out her dagger quickly enough.

"You are not truly here," a rough voice growled, the same that had compelled her to leave and not look back. "Leave me!" He thrust a palm in her direction as though warning her away.

"Grendel." Vynasha moved with every intention of inflicting pain. But she could not lift her feet, could not move at all, she discovered with growing panic.

When she did not move, he turned desperate and shouted at the walls. "She cannot be here! Do you hear me, Mother? I forbid it!" The gatekeeper came to stand arm's-length away from her, still too far away yet close enough she could see regret in his silver eyes and the fresh scrapes along his jaw. He clenched his fists and looked everywhere but at her. "I sent her away, as was my right by your bloody curse." He sucked in a sharp breath and squeezed his lids tightly shut. "Please do not let her in… *do not* let her in."

"How troublesome this must be for you after you sent me away," Vynasha hissed, wishing again for full possession of her limbs. "Why can't I move? Are you doing this, compelling me again?"

He rubbed a hand over his face and let it hang lifelessly at his side. His hair fell into his eyes, and still, he would not look at her. "Not intentionally. This is my dream," he confessed, "though it feels more like a nightmare."

"At least we aren't alone in that." Vynasha narrowed her eyes as all he had and hadn't said ran through her mind, all the tiny ways he'd made her believe she needed to escape while binding their blood. No matter how loudly he protested, she knew he'd used her father to bring her there. He had wanted her there and abandoned her as surely as everyone did.

As you abandoned Wyll to strangers?

Vynasha cringed, and some of her anger slipped away as she asked, "Shouldn't this be my dream? We never shared dreams before." She looked upon her former prison with perverted longing. Why crave such a cold, awful place when she had at last found Ceddrych? Why dwell on this prison when she dreamed of home?

Grendel observed her for a moment, face a mask of stone. "Tell me exactly what you did before you went to bed."

Vynasha snorted. "I'm not your thrall. Why should I tell you anything?"

"Humor an old monster," he said with a slight lift of his chin.

"Not that you care, but Ceddrych found me after I escaped with Grolthox and…" Her words were quickly drowned by Grendel's exclamation.

"Grolthox! He followed you? Damnable creature. I ordered him to remain behind. He should not have been able to make it past the outer wards…"

"Well, thanks to our little blood bond, you aren't the only magick wielder with power over the curse," she spat as her anger flared back to life. Tiny blue lights spun about them in a fine flurry.

Grendel ignored this as he stepped closer, keeping his fists clenched tightly at his sides. "Where is Grolthox now?"

When she couldn't even move to turn her face aside, her temper boiled to a fever pitch. "My *father* is dead."

Grendel blanched and averted his gaze, though his posture remained erect. It was obvious he was aware of Grolthox's true identity when he at last ran an agitated hand through his dark hair.

"What, nothing to say, gatekeeper? You could at least acknowledge you knew he was my father."

His inner light pulsed and then brightened again, illuminating his gray skin as he met her gaze and confessed. "I knew he was your father, and I could not stop him from hunting you."

Her limbs shook, and something snapped in the back of her mind, releasing her limbs. She crossed the remaining distance between them, pulled her hand back, and slapped Grendel in the face.

Dream state or no, she felt the full impact in her aching hand and watched as tiny beads of blue blood rose to the surface of his cheek, where her claws had scratched him.

"He *sold* me to you!" She wrapped her arms around her chest and hung her head until her long hair draped over her face. "And he died saving my life…"

"My father was not a good man, either."

She peeked at him through her veil of curls and pursed her lips. "You don't have any right to mourn with me. He told me what you did to him, Grendel. I can't begin to understand how or why you bothered."

He was silent after that, and the burden weighed on her, threatened to crush her again. Maybe it was being in the reflection of this place that made her add, "I haven't told Ceddrych."

"You said your brother found you?" Grendel took an eager step forward. The lights floating nearby seemed to brighten with intensity, reflecting off his silver irises.

Vynasha took a step back, and the lights around them faded, swallowed by shadow. "Yes."

Grendel turned to pace along the width of the hallway. "Then I am glad. You should both flee these mountains as soon as you are able. Our bond should make it possible."

"Yes, because mortal folk will be so welcoming to a changeling and a woman who looks like a demon," she mumbled with a frustrated sigh.

Grendel continued as though he hadn't heard her barb. "You cannot come here again, not if you don't want her to find you. Never think of me before you sleep again."

"That won't be a problem, gatekeeper," she scoffed. "You made yourself clear when you compelled me to leave."

"Good," he grunted. "Be sure to throw that amulet in the river the first chance you find."

Inky shadows encompassed them, blotting out the moonlight and floating blue lights, and a dull roar accompanied it. "What's happening?" she shouted above the growing din.

Grendel seemed unfazed by the howling winds and hissing voices among them. "It would seem you are waking up." Menace and agony burned behind his eyes, cold and compelling at once. "Do not think of me again, Vynasha."

The last thing she saw clearly was the emptiness in the gatekeeper's masked features. His loss and loneliness resonated with her long after her dream faded to nothing. A voice was waiting for her in the darkness, however, entreating and pulling her back.

*Want to learn more about the world of **Wylder Tales?***
Visit http://wyldertales.com for more!

About the Author

JENNIFER SILVERWOOD has been involved in the publishing world since 2012 and is passionate about supporting the writing community however she can. After studying traditional art at university, she began helping Qamber Designs bring authors' books to life. Jennifer is the founder of We Write Fantasy, a support group for fellow genre authors. She is the author of three series—Wylder Tales, Heaven's Edge Novellas, and the Borderlands Saga—and the stand-alone romance titles *Stay* and *She Walks in Moonlight*.

Discover more about the Borderlands, along with Jennifer's blog on writing life and other bookish delights at www.jennifersilverwood.com.